The AGE-OLD CRIME OF MURDER

Mark Zeid

Manhanset House
Shelter Island Hts., New York 11965-0342

bricktower@aol.com • tech@absolutelyamazingebooks.com
• absolutelyamazingebooks.com

Library of Congress Cataloging-in-Publication Data
Zeid, Mark
The Age-Old Crime of Murder
p. cm.

1. FICTION / Thrillers / Suspense. 2. FICTION / Mystery & Detective / Hard-Boiled. 3. FICTION / Thrillers / Crime. Fiction, I. Title.
ISBN: 978-1-955036-76-4, Trade Paper

September 2024

The AGE-OLD CRIME OF MURDER

Mark Zeid

An Imprint of ABSOLUTELY AMAZING eBOOKS

Habent Sua Fata Libelli

Books by Mark Zeid

Insurance Claims Can Be Murder
Jeff Terrell, Private Investigator, Book One

College Can Be A Killer
Jeff Terrell, Private Investigator, Book Two

Homicide in the Headlines
A Media Murder Mystery, Book One
(A WhoDunIt Award Winner, 2018)

Media Loves Murder and Mayhem
A Media Murder Mystery, Book Two
(A WhoDunIt Award Winner, 2019)

Who's Who in
The Age-Old Crime of Murder

Jennifer Stebbins—29 going on 30, single, and manager of Comfort Cottages, an assisted living facility.

Susan Thompson—young, attractive brunette working at Comfort Cottages.

Fireman William Barlow—third generation firefighter and grandson of Brenda Elson, a resident at Comfort Cottages.

Franklin (Freaky Frankie) Bolen—89-year-old veteran, Marine who served in Korea and Vietnam, real hero with medals, loves baseball, uses a cane. Suffers from dementia.

Leroy Josten—23-year-old black, health care worker at Comfort Cottages, studying for MCAT to enter medical school.

Stanford Agusta—67-year-old detective, served in the army.

Catherine (Cat) Diaz—35-year-old detective, attractive Hispanic woman and Stanford's partner.

Samuel Corden (Smokey—street name)—17-year-old, black, petty thief. Lives with his grandmother who has health issues.

Harry (Haj) Hammar—drug dealer and murderer.

Dorothy Fletcher (Dot)—widower and resident at Comfort Cottages. She uses a wheelchair, loves puzzles.

Brenda Elson—William's grandmother and resident at Comfort Cottages.

Joseph Hamilton—resident at Comfort Cottages. He and Brenda are dating.

Melissa Kelsey—a bit of a snob and a resident at Comfort Cottages.

Denise Linden—25-year-old waitress at Barnyard Barbecue. She has a criminal record for prostitution and possession of drugs.

Firefighter David Richards—friend of William's.

Firefighter Kevin Batters—Air Force vet, crash crew, served two tours in Afghanistan. Also a paramedic.

Firefighter Thom Jacobs—older firefighter counting the days till retirement.

Dr. Robinson—surgeon at the hospital.

Teresa Simpson—Smokey's grandmother.

Valerie Tungson—waitress at Barnyard Barbecue.

Joseph Jacobs (JJ) and Theo Karlow—two thugs Haj hires.

Freya Serban—night cleaning woman at Comfort Cottages. She's from the Ukraine.

CHAPTER ONE

"I'm not crazy," Franklin Bolen kept mumbling to himself as he hurried down the hall. He had to be careful. His 89-year-old legs didn't move as fast as they used to, and he steadied himself with his hands on the wall to ensure he didn't fall. This late at night, it might be hours before anyone in the facility would find him and help him. But he had to find Leroy. Yes, it was late at night, and like many elderly people, he had trouble sleeping. But he wasn't crazy. He didn't imagine it.

"Damn it. Where is that kid?" he muttered when he got to the dining room, the center of the facility where Franklin lived. "Where is that kid?" he shouted, hoping that saying it aloud would answer the question. Several doors opened from rooms down the hall. Residents came out to see who was shouting and why.

As if on cue, Leroy Josten, the attendant who was on duty appeared.

"Where have you been?" Franklin demanded.

"What's happening Frankie?" the young man asked.

"Quit calling me that," Franklin answered with hostility.

Leroy was used to the unorthodox, even hostile, behavior the residents of this assisted living facility had. Still, he was fond of them. They were often bitter and angry, but they also showed him great kindness and support. This was something the 23-year-old, black man appreciated. As for residents making demands at all hours of the night, this was something else Leroy had grown accustomed to. But he liked working nights. It gave him time to study for the MCAT, the entrance exam for medical school. Also, working nights paid a little better than daytime shifts, and he would need the money to pay for medical school if he got in.

"Sorry. Franklin. What can I do for you?"

"You need to call the police. That's what you can do."

"Why do I need to call the police?"

"Because I just saw a girl murdered. Now, call the police!"

Residents were now warily entering the dining area.

"Now calm down," Leroy said as he pulled up a chair for Franklin to sit in. "Where did you see this happen?"

"Quit looking at me like I'm crazy," Franklin insisted as he waved a hand before sitting down. "Call the cops. Some poor girl was just murdered. Out there in the back. Near that dumpster behind that restaurant that you can see from the back of this place. You need to get the cops out there right now."

"Really, you saw a murder?" a resident behind Leroy asked.

"Yes! I did."

Several residents had gathered around the two men and started asking questions. Leroy put up his hand to quiet the few residents that had gathered around. "Frankie, you saw a murder. At night, behind the dumpster at which restaurant? When did this happen?"

"At the one behind us. You can see it from my window. I saw it just now, well, a few minutes ago. It took me a while to find you. And quit calling me Frankie. My name is Franklin. You don't think I know what you all say about me behind my back, but I do. Now, call the cops."

Leroy patted Franklin on his shoulder. "I'll go back there and take a look. If I see anything, I'll call the police." Leroy turned to the others. "Everyone, please stay here."

"You fool," Franklin stood up and yelled. "If you go out there, he'll kill you too. I saw the whole thing from the window in my room. If you want, you can look out my window and you'll see I'm not imagining it. I don't care what you all say. I'm not crazy."

Leroy nodded and left Franklin in the dining area where he was sure Franklin would be okay with several other residents there to look after him. Leroy walked down the hall and entered Franklin's room. He walked over to the window and looked out. He saw the dumpster, but no one was near it. There certainly wasn't a body. He stayed at the window for a moment, staring out at the restaurant's parking lot, searching for any signs of a person in the area. There was a single car in the parking lot; Leroy figured it was probably the janitor's car. He left the room, making sure to close the door behind him.

∞∞∞∞∞∞

Leroy returned to the dining area, surprised to see several of the other residents of the facility and two patrol officers talking to Franklin. Leroy approached the group and asked, "What's going on here?"

"Well, you wouldn't call the police, so I did," Franklin proudly admitted. "And they got here double quick too."

"We were in the area," one of the patrolmen replied. "This gentleman said there was a homicide out back. Do you mind if we check?"

"Not at all, officer," Leroy answered. "But it wasn't in back of here. Franklin said it happened by the dumpster behind the restaurant that is behind us on the next street. I just checked and didn't see anything. But please do check. Maybe it will calm Franklin down."

The two officers nodded in agreement before returning to their vehicle.

"See what you did," Franklin yelled. "You sent them away. They need to check the dumpster. They need to catch the murderer."

"Relax, take it easy," Leroy said as he guided Franklin to a chair and gently forced him to sit down. "They just went over there to check things out. If there is anything, they'll take care of it." A couple of the residents came over to talk to Franklin. This gave Leroy the opportunity to retreat to the front entrance of the dining room, where he could watch the front of the building and residents at the same time. Franklin remained in the dining room with several of the residents waiting for the officers to return. The residents were eager to hear what Franklin had to say. It took less than ten minutes before the patrol officers returned.

One of the officers came into the building to talk to Franklin while the other remained in the car. "We checked out the area around the dumpster. Nothing unusual. Are you sure you saw something out there?" the officer asked Franklin.

"Yes," Franklin adamantly replied as he stood up. "I'm old. I'm not crazy. I'm telling you there was a young woman murdered out there."

"Can you describe the murderer?" the officer asked as he pulled out a small notebook. He noticed the resident spectators were quiet, listening intently to for any details.

"Of course," Franklin answered. "He was medium height and weight, nothing unusual about him except he had short hair, like a military haircut, and weird ears. And he was a white guy."

"Weird ears?" the patrolman said with confusion, looking up from the notes he was writing. "How were they weird?"

"They weren't shaped right. The bottom part was big, a lot bigger than normal."

The patrol office wrote all this down. "How were you able to see all of this from your bedroom window, this late at night?"

"When I saw the woman struggling, I used my camera zoom lens to get a better view. I even took a picture of the guy, but it didn't come out. All you can see is the flash reflecting off the window."

"He's really a very good photographer," said a woman in a terry-cloth robe. "You should see the great job he did with my grandkids pictures."

The police officer nodded to acknowledge the woman's comment before returning his attention to Franklin. "Pretty good thinking for someone surprised this late at night."

Franklin shook his finger at the officer. "Why? Because I'm old. You think because I'm old I can't think, I can't do anything. Well, you're wrong. I'm old, but I'm telling you I saw someone murdered out there. Now do your job and catch the guy who did it."

The police officer put away his notebook. "Tell you what we'll do. We'll patrol the area and keep a sharp eye out for anyone who matches your description. But that's about all we can do."

"What a waste of taxpayers' money," Franklin yelled, waving his hand. "There's a murderer running loose and you're going to patrol the area."

"Thank you, officer," Leroy said interrupting Franklin's rant. "Appreciate you taking the time you took to check things out. I'll take it from here."

"He's all yours, buddy," the officer said as he waved goodbye.

Leroy turned to face Franklin. It was going to be a long night and difficult to get Franklin back to bed along with everyone else.

∞∞∞∞∞∞

"Damn, you're heavy," Harry "Haj" Hammer said to the body of the woman he was carrying. "Damn it. I wish you hadn't done what you did. All you had to do was give it up, but no, not you. You forced me to do this." Haj placed the body on the edge of the ravine and gave it a kick, rolling it down the embankment toward the rocks below. He thought about hiding the body but realized he didn't have enough time. He knew someone would find the body, but he hoped the cops would think she died from falling down the embankment into the ravine and focus on collecting evidence here instead of at the restaurant dumpster where he killed the woman. Also, this would give him time to cover his tracks.

CHAPTER TWO
(day one)

Jennifer Stebbins was an attractive woman with reddish brown hair, a slender figure, and approaching her thirtieth birthday. As usual, she wore jeans and a short-sleeved, printed blouse. Her morning routine was to come into Comfort Cottages, an assisted-living facility, drop off her bag and coat before going to the dining room for coffee and whatever sweet was being served that day. Leroy stopped her before she got her coffee. "Leroy, what's up?" Jennifer asked with a sigh somehow knowing he was going to tell her about some problem or issue with the residents.

"We had a bit of excitement last night."

"What happened?"

Leroy took a quick look around to see if anyone could hear what he had to say. This surprised Jennifer. Leroy stood more than six feet tall and was fairly muscular. She couldn't imagine him being anxious about any of the residents. "Frankie said he saw a woman killed last night." Leroy stated.

"What!" Jennifer shouted. "Why didn't you call me?"

Leroy put up his hands to calm Jennifer down. "The police came and checked it out. Frankie said a man killed a woman by the dumpster at that restaurant behind us. The police sent a patrol unit that checked out the dumpster and found nothing."

"Still, you should have called me, especially when the police are involved."

"Hey," Leroy emphatically said. "This Frankie. His grasp on reality is tenuous. You know he imagines all sorts of things. Half the time he thinks he's still in the Marines fighting in Korea or Vietnam. I mean he's a good guy and everything. But he really doesn't know what is going on most of the time."

Jennifer pounded her thigh with her hand. She turned one way, then another in nervous energy. She held up her hand, signaling for Leroy to stay where he was. Jennifer got herself a cup of coffee and returned to Leroy. "I realize that Franklin is suffering from dementia, but any time any police officer comes here, I really need to be notified."

"It was late at night," Leroy replied. "I didn't think I should bother you because one of the residents had a delusion. I handled it. The police checked it and found nothing."

Jennifer took a deep breath. "You're right. You did handle it, and I know you feel that you did the right thing. I guess I just freak out whenever anything happens that involves the cops."

Leroy nodded. "Hey, I'm black. You're not the only one who freaks out when cops show up."

∞∞∞∞∞∞

"Get out of the way," Dorothy "Dot" Fletcher shouted as she maneuvered her electric wheelchair into the dining room. The eighty-two-year-old widow hated using the wheelchair, but her arthritis limited her walking mobility to only a few feet, just enough for her to get from her bed to the toilet or her wheelchair.

"Now Dot, what's your hurry?" Brenda Elson asked. She was another widow in her eighties.

"Didn't you hear?" Dot replied. "Last night Franklin said he saw someone murdered. I want to get in there and find out if the police have made an arrest."

Brenda smiled at woman in the wheelchair. "I was there last night. Freaky Frankie thought he saw something. Leroy went to check it out and Frankie called the police. They checked it out and it turned out to be nothing. You know as well as I do Frankie has dementia and can be as crazy as a loon. Can't blame him though. I heard he has nightmares because of the time he served in the Marines. My husband was in the Army, and he served in Korea. He never talked about it, but I know it was terrible."

"I was there too. But I don't think Franklin was imagining it," Dot said as she continued into the dining room. "When Franklin gets confused, we can tell. The details don't add up. He gets facts jumbled. He calls us by the names of people used to know, talks about places from his past, he can't remember what he said just a few moments before. But last night, he kept saying the same thing, again and again, to not one person, but to the police and to others. No, I think he actually did see someone murdered."

"Morning ladies," Joseph Hamilton, another resident of the facility, said, smiling at Brenda. "Did you girls have a good night?"

"Who are you calling a girl?" Dot replied. "We are mature women of the world, full of experiences and wisdom."

Joseph winked at Brenda and chuckled. "You women are certainly experienced."

"Quiet, you lecherous old man," Brenda said, playfully slapping Joseph's arm.

"Really?" Dot questioned with a slight tone of disapproval. "What you two are doing is no secret to anyone in this facility. Everyone here knows who is sneaking into who's bedroom in the middle of the night."

Joseph continued to grin. "So, what are you two *ladies* talking about?"

"We're talking about what happened last night with Franklin," Dot answered.

"Why? Who was Franklin with?" Joseph asked.

"Well, after you went to bed," Brenda replied, "Franklin came down to the dining room saying he saw someone murdered."

"Joseph laughed. "That old fart. He was probably watching television and thought it really happened. If he had stayed in his room, he would have seen the cops catch the bad guys."

Brenda glared at Joseph. "Who are you calling an old fart, you old fart? None of us are spring chickens. Besides, being on this side of fifty isn't anything to be ashamed of."

"Honey, we all passed fifty so many years ago, it ain't nothing but a memory," Joseph replied. "So, what did Freaky Frankie say happened?"

"I do wish you wouldn't call him that," said Dot. "He's been through a lot, and having dementia isn't his fault."

"Still, he doesn't have much of a grasp on reality," Joseph countered.

Brenda brought her hand up to her chin. "I know one way we could find out if Frankie really saw what he said he saw."

CHAPTER THREE

Too many people underestimated Stanford Agusta. Too many people saw him as an old black man. He was tall with short, gray hair forming a ring around the bald spot on his head. Too many people were lured into thinking they could fool him because of his soft-spoken and mellow manner. For those who did know Stanford, they knew he was a detective with almost thirty years of experience and several commendations for heroism. Fortunately, Detective Catherine (Cat) Diaz, the 35-year-old, attractive Hispanic woman who was Stanford's partner did.

"What do we have?" Cat asked the patrol office as she and Stanford lifted the crime scene tape over their heads. Stanford and Cat carefully climbed down the embankment to the bottom of the ravine where the body of a young woman laid face up.

"A dead body," the officer answered. "One of the other patrol officers recognized her. Her name is Denise Linden. She's a waitress at Barnyard Barbecue over on Cedar Street."

"Any priors," Standard inquired.

"Don't know," the patrol officer replied. "I can check."

"Don't bother," Cat interjected. "We'll check when we get back to the office. Has the ME been here?"

The patrol officer nodded yes. "We wanted to let you see the scene before they removed the body. The crime scene folks are here. They've already photographed everything. they should be finished up here shortly."

Stanford knelt down to examine the body. He noticed the bruises on her face and the bloody opening on her scalp. There were no other visible signs of trauma except for some blood on her jacket. The victim was dressed in jeans, a white tee shirt, and a velvet jacket with several patches of flags from countries in the Far East. Stanford also noticed the victim was wearing a blue running shoe on her left foot.

"She's wearing only one shoe. Where's the other one?" Stanford said as he stood up.

The patrol officer waved his pen around the immediate area. "We looked for it, but we couldn't find it anywhere."

"There doesn't seem to be much blood," Stanford commented.

The patrol officer shrugged his shoulders. "It could have been absorbed into the ground."

Cat looked around the crime scene. "Who discovered the body?"

The patrol officer pointed to a middle-aged couple standing at the top of the ravine. They were tightly holding a large, active dog straining on his leash. Stanford and Cat climbed up to the couple.

"Good morning," Stanford said as he brought out his police credentials. "I'm Detective Stanford Agusta and this is my partner, Catherine Diaz. Can you tell us how you found the body?'

The man stuck out his hand. "I'm Glen Warren and this is my wife, Alice. We were walking our dog when we saw the young lady down there. I went down to check on her. That's when I knew she was dead."

Cat leaned over to pet the dog wagging his tail and eager to greet Cat. "Great dog. What kind is he?"

"Prue-breed mutt," Alice replied proudly. "We rescued him from the pound. Can't believe anyone would want to give him up, He's so friendly and sweet. But he's ours now."

"When did you find the body?" Stanford asked.

"Well," Glen said while rubbing his chin. "Buddy here wakes us up pretty early to get outside and take care of business. I would say about an hour ago."

Cat pointed to the body at the bottom of the ravine. "There's a shoe missing. Did your dog take it? I can understand if he did, but we do need it if you have it."

"No, ma'am," Glen emphatically replied. "I've seen enough cop shows to know better. When we saw her down there, Alice stayed up here with

Buddy. I went down, to see if she was alive. When I realized she was dead, I came back here, called 9-1-1, waited for you guys to show up."

Cat pulled out her notebook. "How about I get your information in case we need to contact you later? That way you can continue your walk with Buddy. I can see he needs to burn off some energy."

"That he does," Glen answered as he pulled out his wallet to give Cat his driver's license.

CHAPTER FOUR

"Took us long enough," Joseph complained as he, Brenda, and Dot approached the dumpster behind Barnyard Barbecue.

"It's not my fault we had to go around the block," Dot replied. "Besides, it's not like you could have climbed over the fence and down that concrete wall."

"It's not that," Joseph said. "I just mean it took longer than I expected."

Brenda turned her head to glare at Joseph. "What did you think we were going to do? Jog over here?"

Dot looked up at the assisted living facility. "Now that I think about it, it would be a good idea to create a kind of short cut for us to get down here. Then we would have easier access to this area and the restaurants and stores around here."

"Not really," Brenda objected. "That would also give others easier access to us. I've noticed a lot more crime taking place around here in the past few years. That wall and fence make it harder thieves to get in."

"No one is going to come to rob us," Joseph argued, waving his hands toward the facility. "There is always someone there. Why go someplace where you're likely to be caught?"

"Who's going to catch them?" Dot asked. "Most of us can barely walk. We certainly can't chase any criminal down and overpower him."

"But we can pick the thief out from a line-up," Joseph proudly added.

"Only if we have our glasses on," said Brenda.

Joseph snorted at Brenda and looked around the dumpster. He saw a blue shoe lying on the ground. He picked it up and threw it into the dumpster.

"Don't do that," Dot shouted. "Haven't you seen enough police shows to know that you don't disturb a crime scene? You could be destroying valuable evidence."

Joseph held out his arms. "What evidence?"

Dot pointed to a dark stain on the asphalt. "Well, that could be blood. And with DNA, they can tell whose it is."

Joseph turned and glared at Dot. "This isn't a crime scene. Just because Freaky Frankie thinks he saw something doesn't mean a crime was committed. I mean look at this place. Why would anyone want to come here and kill somebody? I know if somebody asked me to meet him in a parking lot by a dumpster, I wouldn't come."

Brenda took out her cell phone and started taking pictures. "What are you doing?" Joseph demanded.

"Photographing the crime scene. Haven't you ever seen anyone do it on TV?"

"While you're at it," Dot said, "get pictures of the cars in the parking lot."

"Why?" Joseph asked with a degree of exasperation in his voice.

Dot pointed to the restaurant. "The only people that should be here are the employees preparing to open the place for lunch. So, if someone did come here to kill someone else last night, then there is a good chance the victim's car is one of these in the parking lot."

∞∞∞∞∞

Haj was pissed. He had to wait an hour before everyone left Denise's apartment building and he was able to get into Denise's apartment. And after spending more than two hours searching the place, he still hadn't found it. After he left Denise's apartment, he drove to a grocery store parking lot down the block from Barnyard Barbecue. He applauded himself for having the foresight to take Denise's keys before dumping her body. He now needed to get her car and move it. He didn't want to leave any kind of trail back to where he had killed her.

He walked into the Barnyard Barbecue parking lot. He stopped. There was an old woman in a wheelchair along with an elderly couple.

Seeing three, old, white people in the parking lot wasn't unusual. But they were taking pictures of the parking lot and of the cars. Haj didn't know who they were, but he knew they were going to cause him problems.

CHAPTER FIVE

"Good morning, Franklin." The cushion made a woosh as Jennifer sat next to him on the vinal couch in the rec room.

Franklin held tight to the remote for the TV. He muted the sound and faced Jennifer. "What do you want?"

Jennifer took a breath. "I understand there was some excitement last night. Do you want to tell me about it?"

"Nothing happened. Why is everyone asking me about last night?"

Jennifer knew it was not uncommon for individuals with Franklin's condition to be unable to remember recent events. "Franklin. Do you remember what you did last night? Do you remember talking to Leroy?"

"Of course, I talk to Leroy. I talk to him all the time. He's a great kid. Did you know that he is studying to get into med school? I hope he makes it. He would be a great doctor."

Jennifer nodded her head in agreement. "Yes, he would. What did you talk about with Leroy last night?"

"Can't remember. Must have been why so many people were out in the halls and the dining room so late. Don't know why they were there, but they were."

"Do you remember seeing a woman last night, maybe in the parking of the restaurant behind us?"

"Quit bothering me," Franklin demanded. "I'm watching the news. I want to find out who won last night's baseball game."

"Okay, Franklin," Jennifer said as she pushed down on the sofa cushion to stand up. She was pleased that Franklin had calmed down. Maybe things would quiet down, but somehow, she knew that wasn't going to happen.

∞∞∞∞∞∞∞∞∞

Less than fifteen minutes later, Susan Thompson, one of the employees of the facility, came running into Jennifer's office. "Jennifer. Come quick. Frankie is losing it."

Jennifer followed Susan into the rec room where Franklin was screaming and pointing to the TV. "That's her! That's her!" he shouted to the other residents in the room. They had backed away from Franklin.

Jennifer grabbed the remote from Franklin and turned off the TV. "What did you do that for?" Franklin screamed. "That's her! That's her!"

"Franklin," Jennifer shouted. "Calm down," she said in a normal voice. "Tell us who she is."

"She's the one I saw," Franklin shouted. "She's the one that was killed."

"You mean the girl you saw last night?" Jennifer asked.

"What?" Franklin replied with confusion. "Last night? What about last night?"

"You said you saw a woman killed last night. Was that the woman?"

"I don't know," Franklin answered. "But I know I saw her killed."

"Where?" asked Jennifer. "Where did this happen?"

Franklin trembled as he glanced at the ground before returning his focus to Jennifer. "I can't remember. But it was dark, very dark."

Jennifer took a deep breath. "Do you remember when you saw the woman? Was it last night?"

"Maybe. I was up last night. I remember because many of us were in the dining room. Leroy was there. He could tell you why we were there."

"Yes, I'm sure Leroy can tell us all about last night," Jennifer said as she guided Franklin back onto the couch. "What can you tell us about the girl? Do you know who she is?"

"No, I don't," Franklin said with a sob. "But I know she's dead."

CHAPTER SIX

Detective Stanford Agusta leaned back in his chair, resting his head against the wall behind him. He stared at the police record of Denise Linden, age twenty-five. Her record showed two arrests for prostitution and one for possession of drugs, but nothing for the past year and a half. Either she cleaned up her act and became a good citizen or she learned to be careful.

Detective Catherine (Cat) Diaz, Stanford's partner, entered the office they shared. Unlike the scenes in TV shows, they had an office to themselves. It was large enough to place their desks facing the door and up against the opposite walls of the office with a large opening between the desks. Along the wall next to the door was a brown, vinal-covered couch. Stanford's half of the office included several photos from when he played football in college and later for the Army. Cat's half had a large cork bulletin board that she decorated with pictures her five-year-old daughter had drawn and several plants.

Cat sat down at her desk and turned to face Stanford. "Checked with motor vehicles and ran her name through the database. Our victim drove a 2020 gray Toyota, license 7121 SHB. She worked at the Barnyard Barbecue. I've also got her address and am waiting on a warrant so that we can search her place."

"What about the coroner's report?" Stanford asked. "Any idea how she was killed?"

"He's not done with autopsy yet, but it looks like blunt force trauma to the head. It could have been from falling down the ravine."

"Maybe."

"I talked to the crime scene unit," Cat added. "They didn't find anything of any real value. No footprints or tire tracks."

"Still, I wonder why she would have been walking along that ravine, alone. Patrol didn't find her car nearby. So, what was she doing out there?"

"Your guess is as good as mine," Cat answered.

Stanford leaned forward and stood up. "Then let's check out where our victim worked. Maybe we can find something there."

Cat didn't respond. She simply stood up and followed Stanford out of the office.

∞∞∞∞∞∞

Stanford pulled the car into an empty parking space at the back of the parking lot of Barnyard Barbecue.

Cat got out on the passenger side and pointed to a car farther down the lot. "Looks like we found Denise's car."

Cat and Stanford walked over to it. Stanford pulled out a nitrile glove and tried the car door. The car was locked. "Looks like we'll have to get a warrant for the car as well as her home," Cat said as she walked around the car, peering in through the windows. "Don't see anything suspicious or signs of violence."

"You know what this means?" Stanford said.

"Yeah," Cat answered. "It means she could have been killed here, or she could have been driven somewhere else and then killed. Either way, it's beginning to look a lot more like a homicide than an accident."

"Going to check on something," Stanford said as he pulled out his cell phone.

While Stanford was talking on his phone, Cat walked around the parking lot. She stopped by the dumpster. She pulled out her phone and took a few photos. Afterwards, she looked in the dumpster. She made note of the blue running shoe she saw in there.

Stanford put up his phone and joined Cat. "Guess what?"

"Que?"

"K?"

"No," answered Cat. "Que. You said guess what and I guessed Que, which is Spanish for 'what'."

Stanford took a deep breath. "Well, you're wrong. I called the desk sergeant. He looked at the call log and said they had a report of someone being attacked back here late last night. This could be where our victim was killed."

Cat pointed to a red stain on the asphalt and one on the dumpster. "Could be. I saw a blue running shoe in the dumpster, kind of matches the one our victim was wearing. The crime scene team isn't going to like us, but we need to get them out here."

"And it gets better."

"How's that?"

Stanford pointed to the assisted living facility at the top of the hill behind the parking lot. "The call came from someone up there. We may have a witness."

CHAPTER SEVEN

It was not unusual for members of the crime scene team to climb into dumpsters to look for evidence. At the same time, it was not something anyone enjoyed doing. They were quick about collecting evidence, mainly because there was so little to find. Everything was contaminated from the garbage and elements. They determined the dark stairs were blood, but whether it came from food items or was human blood would have to be determined later in the lab. The running shoe held some promise of being useful, but again it relied on what they found in the lab. While the crime scene techs finished collecting what they could, Stanford and Cat made their way to the Comfort Cottages Assisted Living Facility.

They were greeted by an attractive young brunette with freckles that highlighted her pale skin. "Welcome. What can I do for you?"

Cat and Stanford took out their identification. "I'm Detective Catherine Diaz and this is my partner Detective Stanford Agusta. We would like to talk to someone about what happened here last night."

"Last night?" the young woman replied. "What happened last night?"

"That's what we're hoping to find out," Cat explained. "Is there someone we can talk to about it?"

"Well, I don't know. This is an assisted living facility and we do have residents here under medical care. Their privacy is a major concern."

Cat smiled. "Excuse me, may I have your name?"

"Susan. Susan Thompson."

"Nice to meet you, Susan," Cat said as she extended her hand. Susan shook Cat's hand. "Listen Susan, we understand your concern about people's privacy. But we are investigating a homicide and it's possible someone here might be able to help us. So, again, could we please speak to someone who can tell us about what happened here last night?"

"Wait here. I'll get Jennifer. She's the manager." Susan disappeared into a suite of offices. She returned a few minutes later, accompanied by another young woman with her reddish-brown hair tied back in a ponytail.

The woman stepped up to the detectives. "I'm Jennifer Stebbins. I'm the manager here at Comfort Cottages. Susan told me you're detectives investigating a homicide. I can assure you no one here has been murdered."

Stanford chuckled. "That's good to hear. We already have one to deal with and we would hate to get another one. According to the dispatch log, there was a call from here last night about someone being attacked in the parking lot of Barnyard Barbecue. Would you know anything about that?"

Jennifer smiled. "Yes. One of our residents thought he saw a woman being attacked last night. He came and found Leroy, the night attendant, who checked it out. But the resident called the police, who I was told, checked it out and found nothing. I'm sorry if this caused your department any trouble."

Cat waved her hand. "No trouble at all. But it turns out the person who called us may have actually witnessed something. If possible, we'd like to talk to him."

Jennifer took a deep breath. "I have no issue with you talking to him. But the resident, Franklin, has dementia. He's not going to be a good witness. He tends to get things confused; he thinks things that happened years ago took place yesterday. Then there are times when he completely forgets what's happened just hours before. You are welcome to talk to him, but I do want to warn you about his condition."

"He's not violent, is he?" Stanford asked.

"Oh no," Susan answered. "He may roar, but he's a real pussycat. Everyone here loves him."

"Susan's right," Jennifer added. "He's harmless. Come on. I'll take you to his room."

Stanford and Cat followed the two women to a large room With the exception of a hospital bed, the room was furnished like a first-class hotel, complete with large screen TV, a comfortable recliner, a desk and chair, a computer, and mini refrigerator.

"Pretty fancy hospital room," Stanford commented.

"This isn't a hospital," Jennifer corrected him. "This is an assisted living facility, and we focus on providing comfortable living conditions for our residents. Franklin isn't here, which means he's probably in the rec room. That's where our residents like to gather and socialize."

The group stepped into the hall when they heard a man shouting, "That's her. I tell you that's her. She was killed."

∞∞∞∞∞∞

Stanford and Cat ran down the hall toward the voice. Jennifer and Susan tried their best to stay caught up with the detectives. Stanford and Cat entered the rec room to see an elderly Caucasian man pointing at the television, shouting. He saw the two detectives rush into the room. "Who are you?" he demanded.

Stanford pulled out his credentials. "I'm Detective Agusta and this is my partner, Detective Diaz. Now, who are you?"

The elderly man stood up to his full height of five feet nine inches. "I'm the one who called the police. What took you so long?"

Jennifer and Susan entered the rec room. They were both out of breath. Jennifer, with her hand on a wall to support her as she caught her breath, pointed to the man. "That's Franklin Bolen. He's the resident who saw a woman being attacked last night."

"That's right," Franklin shouted. "And it's about time you showed up. I called last night and just now you come to find the woman who was killed. If you had been here last night, that woman would still be alive."

A woman wearing a tailored suit approached Stanford. She leaned over and spoke in a low voice. "A patrol unit did come by and check out Franklin's claim about a woman being attacked. They didn't find any evidence of a crime."

Stanford nodded. "Yes, I know. We have a record of the call at the station. Who are you? Did you see anything last night?"

No, she didn't," Franklin shouted. "I was the only one who saw it. But no one believes me. I saw a woman being murdered."

"I believe you," Cat said, hoping to calm Franklin down. "Why don't you tell me all about it?"

"Finally," Franklin said in a huff. "Well, I had trouble sleeping last night. I often have trouble sleeping."

"We all do," the well-dressed woman added.

"Nobody cares about that," Franklin yelled. "Anyway, I was looking out my window, just to see the lights and watch the cars go by on the street behind us. I noticed this couple arguing. Now I couldn't hear what they were saying, but I could tell they were arguing. Then the man grabbed her and started hitting her. I grabbed my camera. I tried to take a picture of them, but the flash went off. All I got was a bright reflection off the window. You would think I would know better. I mean, I've been taking pictures since I was a kid. I know how to use a camera."

"Could you get back to man and the woman arguing," Stanford said, waving his hand in a rolling motion.

"Impatient young fella, aren't you," Franklin responded with an air of indignation. "As I was saying, these two were arguing, but then the guy grabbed the girl and started hitting her. He threw her against the dumpster behind that restaurant back there. He even banged her head against it a couple of times. The woman fell to the ground, but she didn't get up. He killed her."

"Then what happened?" Stanford asked.

"He came into the dining room making all kinds of noise," the well-dressed woman answered. "He woke us all up. That's what happened."

"Oh, shut up, you stuck-up, old prude," Franklin said while waving his hand at her.

Stanford held up his hand, signaling for everyone to quiet down. He turned to the woman. "Ma'am, could you please tell me who you are?"

"I'm Melissa Kelsey," she answered proudly. "My husband, may he rest in peace, was William Kelsey. He was one of the most successful lawyers this town has ever had."

"I knew your husband," Cat stated. "He was a good man."

"That's right. He was," Melissa replied.

"Who cares about your husband," Franklin interrupted. "The police are here to talk to me and find the killer."

Stanford held up his hand again. "Okay. Sir, what can you tell me about the man who attacked the woman? Can you describe him?"

"No, not really. It was dark and I didn't get a good look at him. He was a white guy, nothing special about him except he had weird ears. They were very large at the bottom."

"Weird ears?" said Cat.

"That's right. Weird ears. If my flash hadn't gone off, I could show you."

"That's right," Cat said. "You took a picture of them. Can you show it to us?"

CHAPTER EIGHT

Inside Franklin's room were Stanford, Cat, Jennifer, and Franklin, who was scrolling through the photographs on the memory card in his camera. Standing in Franklin's room, Stanford saw the dumpster in the parking lot of Barnyard Barbecue. Cat patiently allowed Franklin to show her all the photos he had taken in the past few months. She noticed there were lots of pictures of stray cats, which amused her. Turns out Franklin was an animal lover, something he shared with his departed wife.

Finally, Franklin found the photo he had taken the night before. "Here it is. You can't see anything because of the flash. It reflected off the window, so all you see is a bright light."

"Let me take a look," Cat pleaded. Franklin handed her the camera.

Cat turned to Jennifer. "Do you think you could print out a copy of this photo on your computer?"

"Of course," Jennifer replied. "Just give me the memory card and a few minutes."

Cat removed the memory card and handed it to Jennifer. Jennifer exited Franklin's room and made her way through the small crowd of residents in the hallway, all of whom were hoping to find out more about the case.

"See anything?" Stanford asked Cat.

"A lot of cat photos," Cat answered with a chuckle. "But the photo he did take probably won't be of any help. Still, I think a closer look at the picture might be helpful."

Stanford motioned to the dresser. "Looks like you're a baseball fan."

"Sure am," Franklin proudly acknowledged. "Been one since I was a boy. Played in high school. Even made all state, but that was a long time ago."

"Who's your favorite team?"

"Saint Louis Cardinals, of course. Even had an uncle who played with them when I was a boy. He got me free tickets to the games."

Stanford nodded. "That must have been great."

"Sure was," Franklin answered. "How about you? Like the game? Who's your favorite team?"

"Well, since the closest professional team is almost a two-hour drive from here, I tend to watch high school and college baseball. I guess the team I like the most is our high school's team."

"Not the same," Franklin said shaking his head. "Can't get a cold beer or a hot dog at a school's game."

Stanford leaned over and spoke in a low voice. "Some of us have tailgate parties, complete with cold beer, hot dogs, and hamburgers."

Franklin leaned closer to Stanford. "If you ever need a partner for these games, I'm available."

"I'll keep that in mind, partner."

"Partner," Jennifer queried as she returned to Franklin's room. "Just what kind of trouble is Franklin trying to get you into?"

"Nothing that concerns you," Franklin answered.

Jennifer handed Cat a photo printed on copy paper. "Here's the photo you asked for. I made it as large as I could."

Cat studied the photo for a moment before showing it to Stanford.

Stanford saw the middle of the photo was a bright white spot, but around the spot were images of the parking lot. Stanford faced Franklin. "Looks like this photo may be useful after all."

"Why's that?" Franklin asked.

Stanford pointed to the edge of the paper. "You can't see the people, but you can see their legs. One of them is missing a shoe."

"What does that mean?" Jennifer asked.

Stanford pointed to Franklin with his thumb. "It means he really did see someone getting murdered."

CHAPTER NINE

Jennifer returned to her office, thankful the commotion with Franklin was over. She sat down, leaned back in her chair, and closed her eyes, attempting to regain her composure.

"Sorry to interrupt you," a young man said, startling Jennifer. She sat up in her chair to address the stranger. He was in his late 20s, tall, good-looking with a muscular physique. The shadow of a beard stood out against his tan complexion. He obviously didn't work in an office.

"Sorry, it seems I scared you."

"No, not really," Jennifer replied. "I was just trying to catch a breather. There's been a lot happening this morning."

"I know. That's why I wanted to talk to you."

Susan came bursting in. "Oh, I see you found Jennifer. So, what can we do to help you?"

"Before we get too helpful," Jennifer said while motioning to the young man. "Who are you? I don't mean to be rude, but I can't give information about our residents. We do have to protect their privacy."

"I'm William Barlow. My grandmother, Brenda Elson is a patient here."

"Resident," Jennifer corrected.

"That's right," Susan added. "We prefer to call them residents, not patients."

Jennifer stood up and extended her hand to William. "I'm Jennifer Stebbins, the manager. Ms. Elson is your grandmother? Is there a problem with her stay here? We certainly want everyone to be as comfortable and happy as possible."

William shook Jennifer's hand. "My concern is why were the police here? You see, I'm a firefighter. We work closely with the police, so I know a lot of them. I was talking to some of them earlier. We often all go to some fast-food place for breakfast. For most of us, we're getting off duty. My concern is, did something happen last night? I know they responded to a call here. I'm concerned for my grandmother."

Jennifer smiled. "Yes, your grandmother is a pistol. And if I remember correctly, wasn't your grandfather a firefighter?"

"Runs in the family," William answered. "I'm third generation."

"Oh, how exciting," Susan said with enthusiasm.

William faced her. "Not really. Half the time we're doing maintenance and putting out backyard barbecue fires. Still, I wouldn't want to do anything else."

Well, I can tell you that I truly appreciate all that you first responders do," Jennifer said. "We've had the paramedics here a couple of times, and they were great."

"Thank you. But about last night."

Susan put her hands to her chest. "Oh, it was horrible. . ."

"But nothing to be concerned about," Jennifer said interrupting Susan. "One of our residents saw a woman being attacked last night. It happened in the parking lot of a restaurant located behind us. We contacted the police last night and they checked it out but found nothing suspicious. However, this morning, the police did find a woman was killed, and it's possible it happened there. They wanted to talk to the resident who saw it. But I can assure you, our residents are in no danger. I doubt we will see the police again or have anything to do with the case. Your grandmother has nothing to fear."

William chuckled. "My grandmother isn't afraid of anything except forgetting someone's birthday. If anything, I just hope she doesn't cause you any trouble."

Jennifer smiled. "Thank you for the warning. We'll be on the lookout."

CHAPTER TEN

Stanford and Cat had two reasons for returning to Barnyard Barbecue. The first was to get lunch. Their second goal was to find employees who could tell them more about their victim, Denise Linden. Their first objective was successful. The second one was a disappointment. The manager informed Stanford and Cat that Denise was a good worker and dependable. But she worked the night shift and very few people on the day shift really knew her. The detectives would need to come back later to talk to Denise's coworkers. Fortunately, by now the search warrants for the victim's car and home were issued. They were able to get a police tow truck to take Denise's car to the police lot, giving the crime scene techs access to it.

This meant it was mid-afternoon before Stanford and Cat got to Denise's apartment. The dispatcher informed them that no one had notified next of kin yet. A brief conversation with the apartment super revealed Denise lived alone. He followed the detectives upstairs to open Denise's apartment. Stanford thanked him before he and Cat entered the apartment.

Cat picked up Denise's mail from a table in the living room. "Someone's been here," she said.

"Yeah, looks like it," Stanford replied. "Looks like someone was looking for something. The place is a mess. I doubt it was our victim who did this."

Cat looked through Denise's mail before handing it to Stanford. "Here," she said. You get to take care of her bills."

"Why don't you take care of the bills? And while you're at it, see if you can find out who's the next of kin. We still have to notify them. Meanwhile, I'll check the bedroom and bathroom."

"Why don't you take care of the bills and I'll check the bedroom and bathroom?" Cat retorted.

"I'm more likely to recognize evidence of a man's presence, don't you agree?"

"No," Cat shouted. "I'm married with a five-year-old. I'm just as likely to discover evidence of man as you are. In fact, I'm probably better at it than you."

Stanford chuckled. "You're probably right. I'll check the rest of the apartment."

"Good idea. Just stay out of the refrigerator."

"We just had lunch. Now, why would I raid a victim's refrigerator?"

Cat made a face as she left Stanford and began searching the bedroom. The room had been tossed. The closet held blouses, dresses, and jeans. It revealed six purses and a dozen pairs of shoes. None of which were in the closet. Cat searched the dresser, finding nothing out of the ordinary. A search of the bathroom failed to show any signs of the presence of another person.

Cat finished and went to find Stanford, who was in the kitchen reading a magazine and drinking a beer.

I told you to stay out of the refrigerator," Cat said scolding Stanford. "Did you find anything other than a cold beer?"

"Checked the trash. Didn't find anything interesting. Whoever was here looked through everything, but fortunately he didn't trash the place. But I found a note about meeting with someone called 'Smokey.' Don't know who he is or why she needed to meet with him, but she has an appointment with him tonight, at eight o'clock. Unfortunately, it didn't say where."

"Know what I'm thinking?" Denise asked.

"If Denise was scheduled to work tonight, then they're meeting where she works."

"I just hope my husband doesn't get jealous of us going out tonight, because it looks like we have a date."

CHAPTER ELEVEN

"Some date," Stanford said as he and Cat sat in their car in the parking lot of Barnyard Barbecue.

"Well, I didn't expect flowers or chocolate," Cat replied. "I mean, look where we are. We're sitting in a car in a parking lot hoping to find someone called Smokey. Someone who we don't know or have even have a description of what he looks like. How can we hope to find him?"

"With luck. Let's face it, we have a better chance of finding him here than anywhere else."

Cat chuckled. "Talk about luck. Look at what I see."

"Some black kid loitering in the parking lot. He's waiting for someone. Think he could the person we're hoping to find?"

"Could be. If he is, wonder how long he'll wait before leaving."

"Wait here," Stanford said. "I'll go and see if he's the one we're looking for." Stanford stepped out of the vehicle. He walked behind the vehicles in the parking lot, hoping the kid wouldn't notice him until he got closer.

The kid paced back and forth, staying in the shadows as much as he could. He turned and noticed a tall black man coming toward him.

"Evening Smokey," the man said.

Smokey took a step back. "Who are you?"

Stanford continued moving forward. "Someone who needs to talk to you about Denise Linden."

Smokey turned and ran. He ran around the corner of the building with Stanford chasing him. Stanford rounded the corner to find Cat kneeling on the back of the kid.

Stanford put his hand on the building for support. "I'm too old for this."

Cat stood up, pulling Smokey up with her and placing him against the wall. "So, Smokey. What's cooking? I know it ain't barbecue."

"I ain't tell you squat. I don't talk to pigs."

"Then lucky for you," Stanford said, "we're cops."

"No kidding."

"Who are you, kid?" Cat asked.

"Hey, you can't arrest me. I haven't done anything."

"You're a possible suspect in a homicide investigation," Cat answered. "Now. Again. Who are you? I know your mother didn't name you Smokey."

"Homicide! You're arresting me just because I'm black. You have no evidence of me killing anyone because I didn't."

Cat pulled out Smokey's wallet. She removed his driver's license. "According to this, his name is Samuel Corden, age seventeen." Cat continued to search Smokey to ensure he had no weapons. The only thing she found suspicious was a note with the initials DL written on it. The note stated DL had something important.

"So, who are you?" Smokey demanded.

Stanford tapped his chest, then pointed to Cat. "I'm Detective Agusta and that's my partner, Detective Diaz."

"What do you want with me? What? Pin some murder on me because you're too lazy to do your job and find the real killer? So, you pick up the first black kid you can find and pin it on me. Who was I supposed to kill anyway?"

"Denise Linden," Stanford answered. "She was murdered right here in this parking lot last night."

Smokey laughed. "You pigs got the wrong man. I wasn't here last night. In fact, I've got an air-tight alibi."

"Would love to hear it," Stanford stated.

"I was at the hospital with my grandmother. She had an episode. She's asthmatic. I'm sure I'm on lots of security cameras."

"Don't doubt it for a minute," Stanford replied. "What we're interested in is why were you meeting Denise Linden tonight?"

"Who said I was?"

Stanford sighed. "Really? I mentioned the name Denise Linden and you take off running. Now, what am I supposed to think?"

Smokey glared at Stanford. "I don't care what you think."

"Then, why did you run?" Stanford asked.

"I'm black and cops are around. Why do you think I ran?"

Stanford motioned to Cat. "You got him?'

Cat nodded. She placed handcuffs on him to ensure he didn't run away.

"Then I'm going to get the car," Stanford said. "We're going to take a little ride."

"Yeah. Where? To the police station where you can beat me into confessing for a crime I didn't commit?" Smokey struggled in a vain attempt to free himself from the handcuffs.

Stanford pointed to Smokey. "I can't tell you. It'll ruin the surprise."

CHAPTER TWELVE

Several residents of Comfort Cottages were in the rec room, which they quickly abandoned when Stanford and Cat arrived with Smokey in cuffs. Leroy greeted the trio when they entered the main building, attempting to keep the residents from the detectives.

"What's going on?" Leroy asked.

Stanford showed his credentials to Leroy. "I'm Detective Agusta and this is my partner Detective Diaz. Might I ask who you are?"

"I'm Leroy Josten. I'm the night attendant here. What can I do for you?"

"I understand you had a bit of excitement last night," said Stanford.

"Yeah, one of the residents thought he saw someone being attacked. He called the police. They came and checked it out. They didn't find anything."

"That would be a Mr. Franklin Bolen?" Stanford asked.

"That's right," Leroy answered.

"Would it be possible to talk to Mr. Bolen?" Stanford said.

"Why? He's a harmless old man. He didn't do anything."

"Never said he did," Stanford replied. "Still, we need to talk to him."

Leroy nodded. "Okay. Just give me a few minutes to get him."

Leroy left the detectives standing in the foyer. Cat pointed with her chin. "We're attracting a crowd." Stanford gave the crowd a friendly salute.

"What has Freaky Frankie done now?" one of residents inquired.

"Freaky Frankie?" Stanford repeated. "If you mean Mr. Bolen, nothing. We're hoping he can help clear up something."

"Does it have something to do with the murder last night?" another resident asked.

"Sorry," Stanford replied. "Not allowed to comment on active investigations."

"Is he the killer?" the first resident asked.

"That's right," Smokey yelled. "Just blame the black guy. Just because I was in the neighborhood, I must have committed the crime. Don't worry about anything like evidence or anything like that."

Several of the residents fell silent and backed up. "Don't harass the residents here," Leroy commanded as he returned. "They're nice folks, and they don't need you scaring them." Leroy motioned to the detectives. "Frankie, I mean Mr. Bolen will be here in a minute. He wanted to write down what he saw through his camera lens this evening. He uses the camera kind of like a telescope. He's able to zoom in on things with it."

"Don't tell them that," Franklin shouted as he entered the foyer. "You make me sound like a peeping Tom."

"You would be surprised at how useful neighbors who look out their windows are," Stanford said. "Mr. Bolen, I'm Detective Agusta. We spoke to you earlier today."

"I remember," an annoyed Franklin answered. "I'm old but I can certainly remember what happened today. Don't believe me. Go ahead. Ask me what I had for breakfast. I'll tell you what I had. I had pancakes, coffee, and a banana. I'm not senile. I remember you, and your partner, from this morning."

"I believe you," Stanford said interrupting Franklin. Stanford pointed to Smokey. "Have you seen this young man before, maybe one of the times you were looking through your camera?"

"Who is he?" Franklin asked.

"A victim," Smokey shouted. "I was minding my own business when these pigs busted me, just because I'm black."

Franklin took a step forward and stared at Smokey.

"What are you doing?" yelled Smokey. "Ain't you even seen a black man before?"

Franklin ignored Smokey. He turned to face Stanford. "I don't remember seeing him, and I know I didn't see him last night. The man who killed that poor woman was white, and he had weird ears."

"You heard him," Smokey shouted. "The guy you're looking for is white. I'm black. I certainly didn't kill anyone. I had nothing to do with any murder."

"Me thinks thou protests too much," said one of the women residents.

"What are you saying, you old bag?" Smokey said glaring at the woman. "Who are you anyway?"

The woman stepped up to confront Smokey. "I'm Brenda Elson, and I live here. And if you ever talk to me like that again. I will tan your hide. You won't be able to sit down for a month without thinking of me. Didn't your parents teach you to have respect for others, especially in their own home?"

Smokey sneered. "Kiss my . . ."

"Shut up," Leroy shouted, interrupting Smokey. "The lady is right. You really do need to learn some manners." Leroy faced Stanford. "Is there anything else you need from any of us?"

"Stanford shook his head. "Sorry to bother you all."

"It's no problem," Franklin replied. "Anything we can do to help you catch the killer, we're glad to help."

"Meanwhile," Cat said to Smokey, "we're going to the station to have a very interesting conversation."

CHAPTER THIRTEEN

Smokey flipped the bird at the police station as he left the building. Being late at night, Smokey wondered how he would get back to Barnyard Barbecue to pick up his car. He knew there was no way he would get an Uber this late.

"Get in," a voice said from a dark Lincoln sedan.

Startled, Smokey stopped walking. Smokey leaned down, seeing Haj in the driver's seat. "What's up," said Smokey.

"Get in," Haj said again. "I need to talk to you."

Smokey hesitated before getting in the car. He knew the ride wasn't going to be pleasant.

Haj pulled away from the curb. "What did the cops want with you?"

"Nothing," Smokey answered.

"Nothing? They pulled you in and they didn't want anything? Come off it, man. I know better. Now, what did they want?"

"It was about Denise. Did you know she's been killed?"

"Yeah, I knew."

"You did? How?"

"It's my business to know."

"What's up man," Smokey asked as he shifted in the passenger seat of the Haj's car. "I mean, Denise is dead. Then there was that friend of hers, the one who disappeared a month ago. No one knows what happened to her."

"Who cares about her? Now, what did you tell the cops?"

"Nothing," Smokey replied. "They were at the restaurant where Denise works. I was waiting for her when the pigs snatched me. They took me to this old folks' home and asked some old fart if he saw me last night. I wasn't there, so no problem."

"What? What's this about an old folks' home?"

"Turns out this old guy saw something about Denise and what happened to her."

Haj pulled into a parking lot and put the car in park. He grabbed Smokey by the front of his shirt, pulling him closer. "What did this old guy say? Was he able to tell the cops anything?"

"He said he saw a guy attack some woman. I think he saw what happened to Denise. Bummer too."

"What do you mean?" Haj demanded.

"Denise called me the day before yesterday. She said she had something important to tell me. It had something to do with some kind of insurance. We were going to meet last night. That's when the cops got me."

Haj let go of Smokey and pounded the driver's wheel. "Damn it," he shouted.

CHAPTER FOURTEEN
(day two)

"Good morning," Cat said as Stanford entered the office.

"What's so good about it?" Stanford replied. We spent half the night dealing with some punk and got nothing. Any luck on getting a warrant to search his place?"

"Nope," Cat answered. "No probable cause, which is the reason we didn't search Corden's car last night. I'm sorry, I mean Smokey's car."

"The worst part is we wasted a day. We'll have to wait until tonight to talk to our victim's coworkers."

"What?" Cat exclaimed in false surprise. "We're not going out and search for our suspect, a white guy with weird ears?"

"I'm searching for a decent cup of coffee, maybe even three or four to get through the day."

"You're not going to find it here," Cat replied. "But I do have some good news. The autopsy report came in."

"Tell us anything we didn't know?" Stanford asked.

"Not, really. Death was caused by blunt force trauma to the head. She was beaten before she was killed. It was a body dump. No surprise there. The coroner found food particles in the victim's scalp, which came from the garbage surrounding the dumpster. The crime scene techs came back with a report stating the blood they found in the parking lot was human and the same blood type as our victim. But it was too degraded to get any useful DNA results. They went through the victim's car, found some hair, which provided a DNA match to our victim."

"In short, we have a woman beaten to death but no evidence tying her to the killer."

"Well, there is one thing."

"What?" Stanford asked with a groan.

"We didn't find the keys to her car or her purse," Cat answered.

"So, you think the killer might still have them?"

"Bingo," Cat said with glee. "And your prize is you get to buy me coffee."

Stanford let out a low groan. "How did I get so lucky?"

"Oh, you are lucky. Guess where we get to go for the coffee."

∞∞∞∞∞∞

"What are we doing back here?" Stanford asked. "Are you trying to get me into an old folks' home?"

"This is not an old folks' home," Jennifer stated as she approached Stanford and Cat. "This is an assisted living facility dedicated to making residents lives as fulfilling as we can. But I am curious as to why you're back here at Comfort Cottages."

"We got a call from someone here this morning," Cat replied. "A Ms. Dorothy Fletcher said she might have some information concerning the case."

"Dot!" Jennifer exclaimed. "I hardly doubt it. She uses a wheelchair and can barely get around."

"Still, we would like to talk to her," Cat insisted.

"Not a problem," said Jennifer. "Come on. She's in the rec room, probably working on a jigsaw puzzle. She's crazy about them." Jennifer motioned for the detectives to follow her.

While there were several residents in the rec room, most of which were watching a game show on the TV, Dot was at her usual place, a large table with a puzzle spread out over it.

"Good morning," Jennifer said as they approached Dot. "I have a couple of detectives here wanting to talk to you."

Dot looked up from her puzzle. "Do you see any pieces with some orange on them? Growing old means your eyesight isn't as good as it used to be."

Cat pulled up a chair and sat next to Dot. "Let's see if I can find any. You don't mind if I help you with your puzzle, do you?"

"My goodness, no. Love having the company."

Cat looked up at Stanford. "Why don't you see if you can find us a couple cups of coffee while I talk to this lovely lady?"

Stanford nodded. "Best advice I've had today."

"Come on," Jennifer said. "We can go to the dining room. They have coffee, tea, and maybe even a muffin or two left over from breakfast."

Cat watched as Stanford and Jennifer left. She turned her attention to Dot. "So, Ms. Fletcher, what can I do for you today?"

Dot leaned back in her wheelchair. "I hope you know that Franklin really did see that poor girl murdered. He didn't imagine it."

"Yes, we do. We've found evidence that confirms what he told us."

"Good. But what I wanted to talk to you about was that young man you brought in here last night. Is he the killer?'

"We don't believe so," Cat answered.

"But he's involved somehow."

"I'm sorry, but I can't comment on active cases. I'm sure you can understand."

"Honey, I'm old, not stupid."

"I don't doubt that for a minute. Was there anything else you wanted to tell me."

"Of course," Dot answered. "I've seen that young man around before. I often go out behind the building. It's shady out there and there's a nice breeze. It's good to get outside."

"I agree."

"Anyway, I've seen him in the parking lot a couple of times. I noticed him because he stayed in the parking lot, didn't go in to eat. At first, I thought maybe he was looking to break into people's cars, but he kind of stayed in one place. Then a young woman came out to meet him each time. I figured she was his girlfriend, but they didn't act like sweethearts.

They would talk for a minute or two and then she would give him something."

"Do you know what it was?"

"Sorry, no. I thought maybe she was giving him some food, but then I realized if she was, it would be in a bigger bag."

"How often did you see him?"

"Well," Dot said slowly. "I began to notice him several weeks ago. Since then, I guess I've seen him meet up with that woman maybe five or six times."

"Anything else?"

"Well, I did notice one thing that was unusual. Once there was this elderly couple going out to their car. They had a lot of food. He went over and helped them. I think the couple tried to give him a tip for helping them, but he refused it. I was impressed with him being such a nice kid."

Cat nodded. "Can you describe the woman who met with him?"

"Better than that," Dot said proudly. "I know for a fact it was the woman that was killed there the other night. Saw her picture on TV."

CHAPTER FIFTEEN

Jennifer stopped by Walmart on her way home. She paused and looked at the price of eggs. Inflation was really eating away at her income.

"They're pretty expensive, aren't they?" a voice commented from behind her. "I remember less than two years ago they were about a dollar a dozen."

She turned to see William standing there. He was wearing a polo shirt with a firefighter's emblem on it and pushing a cart with several packages of hotdogs and hamburgers. "You must be planning one hell of a barbecue. Or are you going to eat all of that yourself?"

William chuckled. "Hardly. Our section is having a picnic this weekend."

"Really? Just how many people are in your section? That's a lot of meat."

"The picnic is for us and our families. And trust me, between us firefighters and our kids, we'll manage to finish everything off."

Jennifer took another look at William's cart. She noticed other than hotdogs, hamburgers, and buns, there were four cases of beer. "I see you have everything you want, but what about your family? I'm sure your wife will want something for the kids to drink and probably some vegetables."

"I'm not married."

Jennifer smiled. That news pleased her. "Still, I think the other wives would appreciate something for the kids."

"Being taken care of," William replied. "We divided up the shopping lists to make it easier on us."

"Good to know. Well, you take care."

"Wait a minute," William pleaded. "I realize I just met you yesterday, but I was thinking you might like to come to the picnic as my guest. You could save me from having to cook everything."

"Why? You want me to cook everything?"

"Hey, at least I would have an assistant. Come on. What are you doing this Saturday?"

"Where is it and when does it start?"

"High noon at Cedar Park."

"In that case, looks like I'll be at a picnic at Cedar Park this Saturday."

William winked at Jennifer. "Great. I'll save you a hamburger and a beer."

"Looking forward to it," Jennifer replied.

CHAPTER SIXTEEN

"Welcome to Barnyard Barbecue," a cute young woman said to Stanford and Cat as they entered the restaurant. "Will you be dining in, or ordering take out?"

"Dining in," Cat answered before Stanford could say anything. "By the way, is Denise working tonight?"

"Oh, I'm terribly sorry, but no."

"How about her friend?" Cat asked.

The young lady grabbed a couple of menus. "Please follow me." She led Stanford and Cat to a table in the center of the dining room.

"Is Denise's friend working tonight?" Cat asked again.

The young woman placed the menus on the table. "What would you like to drink? We have several soft drinks, all of which are listed on the back of the menu."

"You still haven't answered our question," Stanford said. "Is Denise's friend working tonight?"

The woman looked around before leaning closer to the table and responding in s soft voice. "Denise was killed a couple of nights ago. Look, I don't want any trouble. I've been working here for almost a year now. I can lose my job talking to people about what happened."

Stanford pulled out his badge and credentials. "You're already in trouble. Talk to us and we'll square it with you manager."

"What do you mean?"

Cat signaled that she and Stanford were partners. "We're looking into the death of Denise Linden. We need to talk to her friends. We're hoping they can help us find her killer."

Stanford put away his badge and ID. "Hey, let's make this simple. First, why don't you tell us your name?"

"Valerie. Valerie Tungson."

Stanford clapped his hands together. "Great. Now tell us what you know about Denise. For example, who was she friends with?"

"No one really," Valerie replied. "Most of us are college students, like myself. This is just a part-time job. We have to pay bills and college tuition. Denise wasn't a student, so she really didn't connect with us. I mean, she was friendly and nice, but she didn't hang around anyone here from work."

"Valerie, dear," Cat said in a soothing voice. "She was more than friendly, wasn't she? You all knew her because she was your supplier. She sold drugs, didn't she?"

A look of panic came over Valerie. Cat reached out and took her arm. "We're not here to bust you or anyone for drugs. Tell us about Denise."

Valerie pulled her arm free. "It's not like that. Sure, some of us copped some weed off her, but that's all. I think she might have had something else; you know. But none of us ever did anything."

"Who did?" Stanford asked.

"Look, she took a lot of breaks and went outside. She was usually gone for a few minutes and that's all. It's possible she was selling drugs out of her car. I mean, whenever any of us bought some weed off her, that's where she had it."

"Ever meet any of her customers?" Stanford asked.

"No," Valerie answered. "The only dude I ever saw was this one black guy. I called him the cat man."

"Why the cat man?"

"He was always quiet, watching people. He also had a strange name. Denise called him Smokey. I used to have a gray cat named Smokey. So, I just thought of him as the cat man."

Stanford glanced at Cat. "How often did he come around?"

Valerie shrugged her shoulders. "Don't know. I saw him in the parking lot a couple of times, and once he came inside and ate dinner."

"Did you ever notice any hostility between him and Denise?" Stanford asked.

"Nah. It seemed they always got along. I know sometimes she gave some leftover barbecue. We have to throw it out at the end of the night, so lots of times we take what's leftover home with us. The manager doesn't mind as long as we don't cook anything extra for ourselves."

"One last question," Cat stated. "The other night, the night Denise was killed, did you notice anything unusual?"

"Other than Denise closing the place, no. She usually doesn't do that. It's not a problem. Most of the time a couple of us are happy to do it because it gives us more hours and a chance to earn a little extra."

Cat pulled out a twenty-dollar bill and laid it on the table. "Here's a tip for you; stay away from drugs. Look what it did to Denise." Stanford and Cat got up and left. Valerie stood there until they were out the door. She looked around before quickly grabbing the money.

CHAPTER SEVENTEEN
(day three)

They didn't look like killers. That's why Haj chose them. Joseph Jacobs, also known as JJ, was a veteran and served two tours in Iraq. He served his entire military tour as an admin clerk. He was disappointed that he never saw combat. To make up for that, he decided to learn how to kill in the streets back home. He didn't look like a veteran. He was five feet six inches tall, thin, and always wore Aloha shirts. The other one was Theo Karlow, who looked more like a football player than a killer. Theo made it a point to wear shirts with college logos. However, after a brief conversation with him, people realized Theo probably dropped out of high school and hadn't opened a book since then. Turns out he did have a deadly talent, and just enough smarts not to brag about it. So far, their only real accomplishment was they had managed to avoid being arrested for the four murders they committed.

Haj sat in a booth towards the back of the diner. The breakfast crowd was always only a few people. Most customers came in for to-go orders of coffee and pastries. With free refills and few customers, this proved to be an ideal place to do business that others considered anti-social. A C-note each week to the waitress handling the morning shift ensured Haj always had the same booth in the back. She made sure no one ever sat there, or in any booth near it. Still, Haj made it a habit to check everything on the table in case someone planted any kind of listening device. Haj limited his time at the diner to a couple of hours in the morning, although he did meet others here at other times when needed. The two killers came into the diner, ignored the waitress and went directly to the white guy at the back of the diner. They knew it was him because of the ring in his nose and the two large black discs in his ear lopes. Wearing jeans and a grey tee shirt, Haj looked more like a carpenter than a drug dealer.

"So, why are we here?" JJ asked.

"I thought we could have pancakes," Haj snidely replied.

"The pancakes at IHOP are better," Theo said as he looked around.

"We're not here to eat," JJ responded. He turned his attention to Haj. "What is it you want?'

"Can the attitude. Ever hear of Comfort Cottages?"

Both JJ and Theo shook their heads.

"It's an old folks' home, on Maplewood Drive."

"You're not retiring, are you?" Theo asked.

JJ sighed. "What about the place? Why are you interested in it?"

"You guys know Denise Linden, she's a waitress at the barbecue place on Cedar Street?"

"Yeah, I know her," Theo answered. "I get weed from her sometimes."

"Well, don't get stone while you're working for me."

JJ held up his hand. "Wait a minute. Who said we're working for you? You haven't told us what you want us to do yet."

"It's simple," Haj said. "Two nights ago, Denise had a fatal accident. Turns out there's a witness at that old folks' home. I want you to find him, and make sure he can't testify about what he saw."

"That's a real hassle," JJ said. "Getting into an old folks' home to kill someone. A lot of witnesses."

"For what I'll pay you, you can deal with the hassle and make sure there are no witnesses."

"Two things," JJ said holding up two fingers. "First, how do we find this guy? Do you have a name? Second, what if he dies of natural causes? Do we still get paid."

Haj leaned forward, hunching over the table. "I don't care how he dies. That's between you and God. As for finding out who he is, there's a kid called Smokey. He knows who the guy is."

JJ nodded. "Afterwards, what do we do about this guy Smokey?"

"Use your imagination," Haj answered, smiling.

CHAPTER EIGHTEEN

Smokey knew the man as only *The Accountant*. Once a week, Smokey came to the office on the fourth floor of a medical building. This office wasn't listed on the office directory. The office was just right of the elevator. The sign on the door simply stated *Do Not Enter*. To get through the door, Smokey called the Accountant's phone number. A large man, holding a pistol, would open the door to let Smokey in where two others were waiting. One was The Accountant. The other was the partner to the man with the pistol. No one spoke. Smokey would set a bag containing the money on a desk in front of The Accountant. He would count it, then nod if the count was correct. Smokey wondered what would happen if the count wasn't correct. He was happy he had never found out. Today, the count was correct, but The Accountant didn't nod that it was okay.

"What's wrong?" Smokey asked, trying to hide the anxiety in his voice. "It's all there."

"I know," said The Accountant. "Haj told me he wanted to see you."

"What about?"

The Accountant opened a desk drawer and placed the money inside. "Didn't say. I just know Haj wants to see you."

Smokey looked at the other two men, both of them stood silent. "When" he asked.

"Now," The Accountant replied. "At the diner."

Smokey backed away from The Accountant. One of the other men walked pass him and opened the door. Smokey left without anyone saying a word.

∞∞∞∞∞∞

The waitress realized Smokey was there to see Haj, so she didn't bother with bringing him a menu. Besides, she knew if Haj or his guest wanted anything, they would signal her.

Smokey sat down across from Haj. He placed his hands on the table and started drumming his fingers. "Heard you wanted to see me. What's up?"

Haj remained silent for a moment, more to intimidate Smokey than any other reason. He could see it was working.

"Look," Smokey said a little bit loudly. Several other patrons in the diner turned to see who was talking. Smokey leaned forward and lowered his voice. "Look, it wasn't my fault about Denise, and you know it. She was my friend. I would never hurt her."

Haj held up his hand to silence Smokey. "That's not why I wanted to see you."

"What then?"

"You and her were tight. Did she ever give you anything?"

"Sometimes she gave some leftover barbecue, maybe some extra sauce."

"No, I'm talking about something else. Something she shouldn't have."

"Such as what?"

"A book," Haj said as he leaned forward. "Did she ever give you a book?'

"What kind of book?" a frightened Smokey asked.

"It would be a green notebook. Not very big. Full of numbers."

No, man. She never gave me anything like that.'

"Did she talk about that book?"

Smokey threw up his hands. "Look man. She never gave me a notebook, never talked about a notebook, never even hinted about a notebook. I would show up. She gave me the money, and sometimes she would throw in some food. That's it. I swear. That's it."

Haj leaned back in the booth. "Do you know JJ and Theo?"

"Not really. I've run into them a couple of times. JJ is a posser, always bragging about his military service. I heard he was a clerk in the army.

The closest he got to being wounded was a paper cut. And Theo, he's so dumb, he could get lost in the men's room."

"I don't care what you think of them. I need you to help them do a job for me."

"Forget it, man," Smokey emphatically stated.

"Quiet down," Haj hissed. "I need you to help them find someone."

Smokey leaned forward again, lowering his voice. "Are you kidding. These two couldn't find water if they fell out of a boat in a lake. What are you looking for? I can get it for you."

"I know you can. That's why you're going to help JJ and Theo. You know that old man, the one you said saw Denise being killed. I want you to find him and point him out to JJ and Theo.

"Why?"

"Because I told you to," Haj answered.

"What are JJ and Theo going to do?"

"That's none of your business. Just find the old guy and they will take care of it."

"I don't know. I don't think killing an old guy is a good idea.

"I don't care what you think," Haj growled. "Just point him out JJ and Theo. After that, it's not your problem. Now get out of here."

Smokey slowly stood up. "Okay. But it's a bad idea. I can just feel it in my bones. It's a bad idea." Smokey turned and left before Haj could respond.

CHAPTER NINETEEN
(day five)

Jennifer grabbed a large straw hat as she got out of her car. It was a perfect day for the picnic. It was sunny, but not hot. There was a slight breeze, just enough to be cool, but not uncomfortable. Jennifer could smell the barbecue as she walked toward the large crowd. She stopped for a moment, looking for William. She noticed Dot in her wheelchair. Next to Dot were Brenda and Joseph. Standing behind them was William, who was bringing food for his grandmother and her friends. Surprisingly, Susan Thompson was accompanying William.

"I hope I'm not too late," Jennifer said as she approached the group.

"How wonderful to see you," Brenda replied. She waved her hand toward William. "Let me introduce you to my grandson, William. He's a firefighter just like his father and grandfather."

"She knows that," a blushing William stated. "I'm the one who invited her."

Dot glanced at Jennifer and then William. "You two know each other? Where did you meet?"

"At Comfort Cottages," Jennifer answered. "William came in to ask about Brenda. He wanted to make sure everything was going well for her."

Brenda gently smacked William's arm. "Why didn't you ask me? I could have told you I'm fine. Jennifer and the others take good care of us."

William handed the plates of food he was carrying to Brenda and Joseph. He bent down and gave Brenda a hug. "You weren't around.

Look, I better get back to cooking the burgers and hotdogs before I end up in real trouble."

"Well, be careful. It wouldn't do for a fireman to get burned at a barbecue," Joseph joked.

William gave the group a wave before returning to the grilling area. Susan also gave everyone a wave as she followed William.

Brenda watched the couple leave. She turned to Jennifer. "Well, just don't stand there. Go and get some food. There's plenty to eat. They have enough food to feed a Marine Battalion and still have leftovers. So, don't be shy. Take as much as you want."

Jennifer smiled. "I think I'll get something to drink first."

"Good idea," Joseph responded. "There's lots of cold beer."

"I'll stick with a soft drink for now," Jennifer said. "Can I get anyone anything?"

Joseph held up his can of beer. "I wouldn't say no to another beer." "A 7-UP," Dot chimed in. Brenda waved her hand to signal she didn't want anything.

Jennifer went over to the large barrels full of ice and drinks. She got herself a diet Pepsi as well as the drinks Joseph and Dot requested.

"Now that you got your drink," Brenda said as Jennifer returned to the group, "go and get yourself some food."

Jennifer set her hat and drink down on the picnic table. "Don't worry. I will."

Dot maneuvered her wheelchair to where she was facing Jennifer. "What Brenda wants is for you to go over there and spend some time with her grandson. He was asking about you. And don't let that hussy Susan scare you off. She invited herself when she found out we were coming. She said she was here to take care of us. She's been chasing her grandson like a hound dog after bacon."

Jennifer chuckled and got up. "Maybe I do need to get something to eat." She smiled as she left.

"Tell Susan I need some help with my chair," Dot shouted as Jennifer walked away.

There were four men working at the grill. Susan made it a point to help William, who smiled when Jennifer approached.

William gave Jennifer a salute with the spatula in his hand. "Great. You're here. You can relieve Susan."

"Oh, I don't mind," Susan objected.

"Nonsense," one of the other cooks replied. "We're firefighters, so we're used to the heat. No need for a pretty young thing like you to slave over these hot coals. You go and take a break. You've been here way too long. Go and enjoy yourself."

"Besides," Jennifer added," Dot asked you to come over and help her with her chair."

"What's wrong with her chair?" Susan asked.

"Don't know," Jennifer answered. "She just asked for you as I was coming over."

Susan handed her utensils to William before leaving. The four cooks gave her a wave and said thanks as she walked away.

William handed a pair of tongs to Jennifer. "Glad you came over."

"I came over to get some food and to say hello to the person who invited me and is too busy to spend any time with me. So, I'm left to fend for myself."

"We're here to rescue you darling," answered the oldest cook.

"Let me introduce you to your heroes." William pointed to a black man in his early fifties. "That old guy over there has been fighting fires for almost thirty years."

"Name's Thom Jacobs," he replied. "And in two months, I'm retiring."

"What will you do when you retire?" Jennifer asked as she turned over some hot dogs.

"I can tell you one thing," Thom answered. "I won't be barbecuing."

"He's also the leader of our squad," William stated. "That big muscle-bound guy over there is Kevin Batters. He's an Air Force vet who pulled a couple of tours in Afghanistan."

"Oh, my goodness," Jennifer said with admiration. "What did you do in the Air Force?"

"I was with crash crew, a firefighter on the flight lines. When a plane comes in for a crash landing, we rush out there and rescue the aircrew."

"He's also our paramedic." William waved his spatula at the last man. "That tall, thin guy at the end is David Richards. He and I went to the fire academy together."

"Glad you showed up," David said with a smile. "William was talking about you. Got us all interested in meeting you."

William waved his finger at David signaling him to behave himself. "You're married. Quit hitting on this poor woman. Besides, your wife is over there with the other wives and their kids."

"Do you have any children of your own?" Jennifer asked.

"Not yet," David answered. "But we hope to. How about you?"

Jennifer turned and bowed. "Nope. Single and free."

"She's perfect for you William," David yelled.

William blushed. "Do you mind if we wait until after she's had some food before we talk about dating?"

"Don't mind at all," Thom replied as he picked up a plate and piled two cheeseburgers on it. He handed the plate to Jennifer and pointed with his spatula. "All the fixings are over there. You go and get whatever you want." Thom then grabbed the spatula from William. "And you go over there and join her."

CHAPTER TWENTY
(day seven)

"Jennifer, Oh Jennifer," Brenda called out. "I need to talk to you."

Jennifer stopped outside of her office. It was Monday morning, and she was hoping her week wouldn't start out with a problem. "Let me put my coffee down first, then I can help you." She stepped into her office and placed her coffee on her desk. She turned and took a deep breath to brace herself for whatever issue Brenda was bringing her.

"Did you enjoy the barbecue? I hope you got to spend some time with William."

"Yes, I did, to both questions."

"I noticed Susan wasn't too happy to see you and William together," Brenda said. "By the way, did you have breakfast? They still have some muffins left over from this morning."

Jennifer began to relax. Maybe, she thought, there isn't going to be any kind of trouble. "I'm fine, thank you. So, what did you want to talk to me about?"

Brenda moved closer to Jennifer. "It's about that poor girl that was murdered. Have you heard anything more about it? Have they caught the killer?"

"Brenda, the police aren't going to tell me anything. Why should they? I . . . we have nothing to do with it. We didn't know the victim, or the killer, or the reason why."

"Shouldn't we do something to help them?"

"Do what? No one here has any experience in dealing with a homicide," Jennifer said as she thrust her hands out in front of her.

"Let's face it. Half of our residents have trouble finding their eyeglasses. They certainly can't help the police find a killer."

"How can you say that?" Brenda exclaimed. "Why? Because we're old? You think we're incapable of doing anything?"

"No. No. It just that the police have resources, we don't. Besides, even if we somehow do find the killer, what can we do? This person killed one person. He certainly won't think twice about killing any of us. Getting involved is dangerous."

"And remaining silent is just as bad," Brenda stated before she stormed off.

Jennifer sighed. She was wrong. There was going to be a problem.

∞∞∞∞∞∞

Joseph snuck up behind Brenda and put his hands on her shoulders. "Hey hot stuff. What's happening?"

Brenda shook Joseph's hands off her shoulders. "Don't hot stuff me. I'm mad."

Joseph took a step back. "What did I do?"

"Nothing. I'm mad at Jennifer."

"Why?"

"I was talking to her about us helping the police with finding the killer of that poor girl. But Jennifer thinks we're a bunch of old folks who should be sitting in rocking chairs waiting to die."

Joseph shook his head. "I'm sure she doesn't think that. Look at all the outings and activities she plans for us. She makes sure we're taken care of. We're free to come and go as we please."

"That's right, and right now I'm going to find the killer of that woman. All I have to do is figure out how to do it."

"Well, don't ask me. I don't know what to do," Joseph said. "The closest I ever came to any criminal activity is pulling some pranks on Halloween when I was a teenager. I don't even know anyone who has committed a crime."

"We don't want a criminal. We need to find someone who knows how criminals work."

"We could talk to Melissa. Her husband was a lawyer. She probably knows how to find a killer. I'm sure her husband dealt with some."

"I don't know," Brenda said pouting. "She's a bit of a snob. She thinks just because she had money, she's better than us. But look where she is. She's here with the rest of us."

"Do you have a better idea?"

"No," Brenda relented.

∞∞∞∞∞

"Hey, Melissa," Joseph said as he and Brenda approached Melissa in the rec room talking to Dot over a jigsaw puzzle. "How are you doing?"

"Quite well, thank you," Melissa responded. "How about you and Brenda? Are you doing well?"

"Fit as a fiddle and raring to go."

"Go where?" Dot asked.

Brenda took a seat at the table where the puzzle was. "I was talking to Jennifer about that poor girl that Franklin saw murdered."

"Yes, it was dreadful," Melissa said. "I wish there was something we could do, perhaps we could reach out to her family."

"What a great idea," Dot said. "Maybe we could send some flowers. I'm sure the family would appreciate it."

Melissa nodded. "I agree. Flowers would be nice."

"Yes, they would be," Brenda replied. "But I was thinking of something else. I was thinking maybe we could help the police catch the killer."

"Oh, my goodness," Melissa responded. "How are we going to catch a killer? None of us have any police experience."

Joseph pointed to Melissa. "We were thinking maybe you know how. Your husband was a lawyer. Certainly, he dealt with a few criminal types. I'm sure you picked up a few things from him on how criminals think."

Melissa gave Joseph a disapproving look. "My husband was a tax attorney. And the only criminal he ever dealt with was the one who lost our money. We ended up with almost nothing while he got rich. So, the only advice I can give you about crooks is never believe a word they say."

"Now, now," Dot said patting Melissa's hand. "I'm sure Joseph didn't mean any disrespect."

"No, no. I didn't," Joseph added. "What I meant was you probably knew who we could talk to about how to help the police."

"I don't know anything about solving a crime," replied Melissa.

"Well, I have read a lot of mysteries," Dot said. "I know there has to be a reason for killing someone. Since the woman was beaten to death, I think maybe the murder wasn't planned. I mean if it was planned, wouldn't be easier to kill her with a gun or something instead of beating her. So, the first thing to figure out is the motive."

"Great," Brenda shouted. "How do we do that?"

"Well," Melissa said slowly as she looked at the three individuals surrounding her. "I would think you would need to find out all you can about this woman and her life. What did she do? Who were her friends? Did she have lovers? Etc. It would also be useful to see what the police have uncovered so far."

"We can start with talking to people at the restaurant," Brenda said with excitement. "I'm sure they know all about the woman."

"Why not," Dot asked. We could go over there for lunch or dinner and talk to the people there. We'll have to take Franklin with us."

"What?" shouted Joseph. "Take Freaky Frankie with us. Why?"

"His name is Franklin, not Freaky Frankie," Dot admonished Joseph. "What if the man who killed the woman works there? Franklin is the only person who can identify him."

CHAPTER TWENTY-ONE

"This is a great idea," Franklin said as he tried skipping while holding onto his cane. "I love going out for lunch."

Brenda shushed him. "Quiet. We don't to attract attention."

"Relax," Dot said as she moved her wheelchair toward the door of the restaurant. "As far as anyone knows, we're here for lunch."

Joseph leaned over and spoke in a low voice. "Let's just hope Freaky Frankie doesn't lose it if he sees the killer."

Melissa glared at Joseph and moved up to take Franklin's arm. Before anyone entered the restaurant, she turned to face the others. "Remember our goal is to find out what kind of person Denise Linden was."

"That's the woman Franklin saw killed," Dot reminded everyone.

"Don't you worry," said Franklin. "If I see the person, who did it, I'll let you all know."

"Oh, good grief," Melissa said as she motioned for Joseph to open the door.

"Welcome to Barnyard Barbecue," said a young woman wearing jeans and a red and white checkers shirt. "Five for the dining room?"

"That's right," Franklin replied with enthusiasm.

"Follow me," the young woman said.

Joseph smiled and said, "Gladly." Brenda smacked him in the arm.

The hostess led the group to a large round table. She laid menus in front of each guest. "My name is Valerie and I will be your waitress today. Our lunch special today is a pulled pork sandwich with your choice of cole slaw, potato salad or French fries along with a soft drink.

Of course, you may order anything from our lunch menu if you prefer. I'll give you all a moment to look over the menu."

"Do you think she knows anything about the girl that was murdered?" Joseph asked as the hostess walked away.

"Please," Melissa responded. "Let me ask the questions. The key here is to be discrete."

"You don't think we can be discrete?" Brenda said snidely.

Melissa took a deep breath. "My dear. I'm sure you can be discrete, but I'm afraid your enthusiasm may alert the very person we are looking for. Remember, we're here to find a killer. It's best he doesn't know we're looking for him. Now, I suggest everyone make their selection for lunch."

The group enjoyed their lunch. While Franklin and Joseph managed to get sauce on their shirts, the ladies did not, although Dot limited her lunch to a salad and a piece of peach pie. The waitress came by. "Will that be separate checks?"

"No dear," Melissa answered. "Put it all on one check. We'll figure out who owes what later. We all live behind you in Comfort Cottages."

"Well, that makes my job easier," Valerie happily replied.

Melissa put her hand on Valerie's arm. "But we do have one favor to ask you, my dear. We heard about the poor woman who was killed here last week. Did you know her?"

"Yeah," Valerie answered. "Her name was Denise. She works nights. I'm usually on nights, but now I work days. I mean I knew her, and she was nice."

"Well, the reason I asked is we would like to send some flowers to the family. We really do want to pay our respects to her family. Do you know where we could send them?"

Valerie shrugged her shoulders. "Sorry, but no. I didn't know her that well. But if you leave me your name and contact info, I can let the manager know and he can contact the family for you. Even if I did know Denise's address, I couldn't give it out."

"Of course not, dear," Melissa said with understanding. "You must protect her privacy. But maybe you could have one of her friends contact us and we could have that person deliver the flowers for us."

"Yeah, I can do that. Just write down you name and info."

Melissa pulled a piece of paper from her purse and took the pen from Valerie. "Thank you, my dear. This is really very sweet of you."

∞∞∞∞∞∞

Smokey sat in the back of the black Ford sedan with JJ and Theo in the front seat. "What are we doing?" Smokey complained. "We can't keep going around the neighborhood, hoping the old man is going to come out. It's not like he's going to be walking a dog."

"Want to go inside that old folks' home?" JJ asked.

"Are you nuts," Smokey shouted. "They know me in there. I can't go in and ask to see the old man who talked to the police."

"Do you have a better idea than driving around?" JJ said looking at Smokey in the rear-view mirror.

"Maybe one of you could pretend you're delivering a pizza and have the wrong address. Then you could plant a small video camera somewhere. When I see him, I can point him out to you."

JJ turned around to face Smokey. "How do we manage to get in and plant a camera, which needs to be hidden, without attracting attention?"

"Good point," Smokey conceded.

"Hey," Theo said pointing out the window, "maybe it's one of them."

Smokey scooted forward to get a better look. "Lucky us. It is. It's the old guy with the cane. The one behind the woman in the wheelchair."

"Hey," Theo said with a smile. "It worked."

CHAPTER TWENTY-TWO

"There are a lot of forms," JJ said as he looked through the package Jennifer had given him. He held the forms in his hand as he twisted around in the chair. Being in Jennifer's office limited his chances of finding his target.

"I realize that," Jennifer replied from behind her desk. "But to provide the best possible care for our residents, we need a full medical history and personal background. We want our residents to be happy as well as healthy."

JJ continued to look through the forms. "You know, if my grandma was healthy, I wouldn't have to put her in an old folks' home."

"We prefer to call it an assisted living facility. We not only look after our residents' medical and health issues but provide a social environment for them. Perhaps you could tell me the issues your grandmother is having."

JJ waved his hands. "She's a bit crazy. She can't remember things. Often, she gets lost and wanders around the neighborhood looking for people who aren't there. I need to be sure someone will look after her and keep her safe."

"I can understand your concerns," Jennifer replied. "We do provide for all our residents' needs. We have an exercise room, a rec room, social activities, and bus service to local shopping centers and parks. Our residents are also allowed to go and come freely to visit places and people on their own. For those who need someone to ensure their safety, we do provide that also."

"How do you do that?"

"We can provide a kind of beeper. It gives us the location of the individual when it is on their person. Also, we know which residents need extra care for their safety. The entire staff is aware of who they are and we all tend to keep a close eye on them. Even many of the other residents look after each other when necessary."

"Any chance I can get a look around?" JJ asked.

"Of course. We welcome family members to tour and check out our facilities. Let me get someone to guide you."

"Thanks," JJ replied.

Jennifer had Susan take JJ around the facility. JJ pretended interest in the facility, stopping at the rec room. "Do they always come here to watch TV?"

"Not really," Susan answered. "Most of them come here to watch movies on DVD or Blu-ray. I think the residents come here to meet and talk to each other. If they just wanted to watch TV, they would stay in their rooms."

"Can I talk to some of the people here?"

"Sure. They love to meet visitors."

JJ approached a woman in a wheelchair. Next, he talked to a man with a cane. After chatting with a few other residents, he returned to Susan.

"Hey, this place seems okay," JJ commented. "I kind of like the place. I think I'll talk to Grandma about coming here. Thanks for the tour."

Susan escorted JJ to the exit. She watched as he got into his car and left.

∞∞∞∞∞∞

Ten minutes later JJ pulled into the parking lot of the diner where he had met Haj. He found Theo and Smokey in a booth. He took a seat next to Theo. "I found the old guy."

"Hey, I found the old guy," Smokey said.

"Yeah, but I found him in the old folks' home. His name is Franklin Bolen. He's suffering from dementia. But Haj is right to be concerned. The old guy did see him kill the girl. He can't stop talking about it. He thinks he's some kind of hero because he called the police. What's worse, he's got several of the others there working with him trying to find Haj. They think it's game."

"He named Haj?"

JJ shook his head. "No, but he described the person who killed that girl. It's Haj all right."

"Yeah, but what are we going to do?" Smokey asked.

"You do nothing," JJ answered. "We can't have you hanging around there. Theo and I will take care of the old man. But hang loose in case we need you for something."

"When are you going to it?" Smokey asked.

"That's something you don't need to know."

CHAPTER TWENTY-THREE

Theo turned off the headlights as he pulled into the parking lot of Comfort Cottages. This late at night, Theo knew the lights would attract more attention than any engine noise. He thought about parking in a dark corner, but he chose to park near the exit instead. He and JJ got out of their car. They waited for several minutes to see if anyone would come out of the main building. There was no noise or any movement. They entered the building as quietly as they could.

Theo motioned toward a young black man studying some books. "How do we get pass him?"

JJ put his finger to his lips. "I want you to count to twenty. Then walk to the center of the room. I'll take him out while he's watching you." JJ moved quietly to hide behind a pillar. Theo counted and walked to the center of the room.

The movement of Theo walking into the room attracted Leroy's attention. He closed his books and got up from his desk. "Who are you?" Leroy demanded.

Theo looked at the black man addressing him. "I'm here to visit my aunt."

"A bit late to be visiting," Leroy replied as he left his desk. "Again. Who are you and who is your aunt?"

JJ picked up a chair and brought it down on the back of Leroy's head. Leroy fell to the floor. He shook his head and started to get up. JJ kicked Leroy in his side. Leroy rolled over. Before Leroy could do anything, JJ grabbed Leroy's head and banged it against the floor, ensuring he lost consciousness. Theo and JJ stood over Leroy.

"Think he's dead?" Theo asked.

"Doesn't matter," JJ answered. "Let's get that old man and get out of here."

∞∞∞∞∞∞

Freya Serban pushed her cleaning cart out of the women's restroom. The time she spent in Ukraine when the Russia invaded, forcing her to flee to the United States, gave her a sixth sense of danger. Night was always the worse back then; that's when the soldiers would come to steal and attack women. As she moved down the hall, pushing her cleaning cart, that sixth sense came back to her.

∞∞∞∞∞∞

"Man, am I stupid," Smokey said to himself as he climbed the embankment to the fence behind Comfort Cottages. "What am I doing here?" as he continued talking to himself. He climbed over the fence and snuck up to the back of the main building. Crouching along the side of the building, hoping no one would look out their windows, he moved to the parking lot in front of the facility. Smokey saw Theo's car, but no sign of JJ or Theo. Again, Smokey asked himself why he was here.

∞∞∞∞∞∞

"How are we going to find that old man?" Theo asked as he and JJ walked down the hall. "We don't know which room he's in."

"Well, if we can't go to him," JJ answered, "we'll have to get him to come to us." JJ pointed to the wall. Theo signaled he understood.

∞∞∞∞∞∞

Fear was a constant companion for Freya during those months she spent in the bunkers, hiding from the Russian shelling of her hometown. She knew that hiding from threats only allowed them to grow. The fire alarm startled Freya. Somehow, she knew the alarm was a diversion and the real danger was yet to be revealed. She grabbed the only weapon she had, a spray bottle of cleaner. Terrified, with her hand on the wall to steady her, she moved forward, knowing she had to face the danger lurking down the hallway.

CHAPTER TWENTY-FOUR

Franklin woke up, confused, and startled. The alarm ringing throughout the building was bringing the residents out of their rooms, many of them pulling on robes or wrapping blankets around their shoulders. "What's going on?" yelled one of the residents.

∞∞∞∞∞∞

Dot came out of her room, hugging the wall, annoyed at being awakened by the ringing alarm. Fear overwhelmed her; she needed to get to her wheelchair, which was still in her room. It was the only way she could escape the danger. She realized someone had set off the fire alarm. She took a moment to look around trying to find out where the danger was. There was no sign of smoke or fire. This caused Dot more anxiety. She hoped this was a case where one of the residents burnt their microwave popcorn and panicked.

∞∞∞∞∞∞

JJ and Theo stood against the wall, watching residents. An old woman, frightened, came out of her room. She stood there, hugging the wall, and upset at the disturbance. Theo grabbed the woman and shoved her back into her room. Before she could react, Theo forced her onto her bed. He brought out a sock filled with rocks. JJ stopped Theo from hitting her.

"Just tie her up," JJ said. "Then blindfold and gag her. She won't be any trouble.

"How do you know?" Theo asked.

JJ pointed to the wheelchair.

Theo grabbed the belt from Dot's robe and did as JJ instructed while JJ kept watch at the door. He kept it mostly closed, just opened a crack to see into the hallway. Residents were milling around, confused, unsure of what to do. One of them shouted they should go to the front of the building. The residents began moving in that direction. JJ motioned for Theo to join him at the door. JJ pointed to an old man walking down the hall, steadying himself with his hand on the wall. They found their prey.

∞∞∞∞∞∞

Freya started herding the residents to the front of the building. The act of taking care of these people gave her courage. She would gently guide individuals toward the dining hall where they could gather and find out what was happening. She saw Franklin, with his hand on the wall, walking slowly. Freya started toward him.

∞∞∞∞∞∞

Theo rushed out of the room where he and JJ were hiding. He grabbed Franklin, putting one hand over Franklin's mouth and lifting Franklin up with the other arm. JJ ran out of the room, shutting the door. He grabbed Franklin's arm. With Theo on one side and JJ on the other, they turned Franklin around. After a quick glance backwards, they started down the hall, away from the others. The only obstacle in their way was a woman with a spray bottle.

∞∞∞∞∞∞

Freya had seen this before, when soldiers and criminals would abduct someone for either money or sadistic pleasure. She was not going to let this happen here. She stood firm and raised the only weapon she had. The two men dragging the old man stopped a few feet in front of Freya.

Theo chuckled at the idea of being threatened by a spray bottle. Freya pointed it at Theo and squeezed the trigger, spraying a cleaning solution in Theo's face. Theo screamed. JJ let go of Franklin and took a step toward Freya before she sprayed JJ in the face. While the two men were trying to wipe the solution from their eye, Freya grabbed Franklin and dragged him away from them.

∞∞∞∞∞∞

The fire alarm startled Smokey. For an instant, he stood there in the parking lot, trying to convince himself he should go into the facility to see if any of the aged residents needed help. "It's not my problem," he said to himself as he took a few steps away from the building. He heard some of the people moving about inside the building. He stopped, turned, and ran inside, cussing himself for being a good Samaritan.

∞∞∞∞∞∞

The first person Smokey saw upon entering the facility was a black man lying on the floor. Smokey stooped down to check on the person. The man groaned. Smokey looked up to see several elderly people in pajamas and robes.

"He's killed Leroy," one aged woman shouted. Another woman screamed.

"No, no," Smokey yelled. "I found him like this. I didn't do it." Sirens drowned out Smokey's replies. Flashing lights lit up the outside and the entrance to the facility. Smokey stood up, took a quick look around, and ran down a hallway away from the lights and the crowd. He kept looking over his shoulder to see if anyone was chasing him. He should have been looking where he was going. He literally ran into Theo. For Smokey it was like running into a wall, knocking Smokey to the floor.

JJ kept wiping his eyes, bringing his vision into focus. Through blurred vision he recognized Smokey. "What the hell are you doing here," JJ yelled.

Smokey crawled backwards on the floor. "I thought you might need some help."

"Where's the old man?" Theo demanded.

Smokey managed to get to his feet. "I think some woman was taking him to the police.

"The police," JJ shouted. "The police are here?"

Smokey nodded yes. "I heard sirens and saw the lights out front. The cops are coming. We have to get out of here."

JJ signaled for Theo and Smokey to follow him. "Let's see if we can get out the back."

∞∞∞∞∞∞

William was the first firefighter off the truck, rushing in while the other three firefighters; David Richards, Kevin Batters, and Thom Jacobs were getting gear off the truck. "Hold up," Thom yelled after William. "We don't know what to expect."

William ignored him and ran through the front door.

∞∞∞∞∞∞

Dorothy (Dot) Fletcher was angry. First there was that damn alarm waking her up. Then there were those two thugs who grabbed her and tied her up. She knew they were two men, but it happened so fast, she barely saw them. It was just a blur, one short guy and a much larger one. To make matters worse, it took her several minutes to get herself untied. The alarm was still going off. Dot heaved herself into her wheelchair, opened her door and saw three men running down the hall. She recognized the last person in the group.

∞∞∞∞∞∞

"Quiet down everyone," Brenda shouted. She grabbed a chair to help her get down to the floor. She leaned over Leroy and placed her fingers on his neck. "I think he's alive," she said.

"We need to call an ambulance," Joseph said to the crowd of residents that had gathered. One of the residents pointed to the office. Joseph pushed his way through the group. He picked up the phone receiver.

∞∞∞∞∞∞

William saw the group of residents standing around a person on the ground, however his attention was focused on his grandmother, Brenda Elson.

"William!" she shouted. "Thank goodness you're here." Brenda pointed to Leroy who was still on the floor. "You've got to help him."

"What's going on here?" Thom, the senior firefighter, demanded as the other two firefighters, David and Kevin knelt down to care for Leroy.

Joseph held his palms up. "We don't know. The alarm went off and we all came out of our rooms. When we got here, we found Leroy. Is he dead? Can't you do something?"

"He's not dead," Kevin answered. "Looks like he was knocked out. We'll take him in as soon as we can. Where's the fire?"

"What fire?" Brenda yelled. There's a fire!"

∞∞∞∞∞∞

Dot in her wheelchair hurried down the hall, catching up with Freya and Franklin. She followed Franklin and Freya to the front of the building. The three of them entered the room. She saw the firefighters. Realizing what was going on, she pushed her chair forward. "There's no fire," she shouted.

"Then who pulled the fire alarm?" an angry William demanded. "What's going on here? Are you guys so bored that you get your kicks from calling us out in the middle of the night?"

Freya helped Franklin to a chair. "No one here pulled the alarm. It was one of those kids."

"What kids?" William asked.

Dot pointed down the hall. "There were three of them. Two of them burst into my room and tied me up. They were waiting for something. After they left, I was able to get free. When I left my room, I saw three of them running out the back way."

William brought a small notebook out of his pocket. "Can you describe them?"

"Better than that," Dot proudly stated, "I recognized one of them."

CHAPTER TWENTY-FIVE

No matter how often Jennifer came to the hospital, it never got easier for her. The noises of doors opening, groaning patients on gurneys being wheeled to destinations, and the cries of fear and sorrow from family members made the hospital a place of despair instead of one of hope. Her visits centered around residents dealing with major, often life-threatening illnesses or accidents. And too often, these visits ended with the death of the victim. This time Jennifer was comforted to discover William was at the ER.

"What brings you here?" William asked.

"Really," Jennifer said with anger and fear in her voice. "Leroy was beaten and is in the hospital. Of course, I'm going to come down here to check on him."

"It's the middle of the night. You should be sleeping."

"So should you," Jennifer said, gently jabbing William with her finger. Touching him calmed her, giving her a sense of safety "Don't you get to sleep at night?"

"We do if there isn't a fire, or if someone doesn't pull the fire alarm."

"Yeah, I heard about that."

"You know what happened?"

"Not quite."

William guided Jennifer to some chairs in the waiting room. She welcomed the feel of his hand on her back. "Some men came into the facility. One of them pulled the alarm to get the people out of their rooms. Then they went after this one guy. But your cleaning lady ran into them and sprayed them with her cleaning solution. When they let go of the guy they were holding, she grabbed him, and they got away.

When we arrived, the guys who pulled the alarm ran out of the back of the building. But luckily, one of ladies living there recognized one of them."

"Who was it?"

William shrugged his shoulders. "Don't know. The lady who saw them talked to the police, but they didn't tell us. So now, we're checking all the local ERs to see if anyone has come in with some kind of eye problem."

"How's that going?"

"So far, all we've managed to do is lose a lot of sleep."

"Oh, my goodness," Jennifer said. "Tomorrow's going to be a rough day for you."

"Not really. We get off at eight in the morning. We can sleep after that."

Jennifer smiled and put her hand on William's arm. "Well, it's going to be a rough day for me. But if you and your friends want to stop by after you get off, I'll make sure we have some coffee and sweets for you."

"What makes you think we won't just go home and to bed?" a voice behind Jennifer said.

She turned to see Thom, the leader of William's team. "If that were the case, you wouldn't be spending the night checking all of the ERs in the area."

"Busted," Thom replied.

"In that case, I wish you all the best of luck," Jennifer said as she rubbed her hand along William's arm.

William smiled and gave Jennifer a quick kiss before he left. She blushed but wished the kiss had been longer.

∞∞∞∞∞

Police interview rooms aren't like they are on television. They are barren, nothing on the walls to distract the person being interviewed. There used to be a large two-way mirror, but now more often cameras are used to record and observe what goes on in the room. Instead of a table, with chairs across the table from each other in the center of the room, the table is usually in a corner with chairs on the adjoining sides. Investigators know it's their people skills, their ability to connect with the person being interviewed, that leads to solving crimes. Being adversarial tends to put others on the defensive and they tend to clam up. But one thing does work. Leaving a person in the room alone for some time causes the individual to become nervous. This often gives the investigator an advantage. Smokey was in the room for twenty minutes before Detective Cat Diaz walked in.

"Why am I here?" Smokey demanded, pounding the table with his finger.

"Last night there was an incident at Comfort Cottages," Cat explained as she sat down. "Someone said you were one of the three people there who caused the problem."

"I didn't hit that dude," Smokey shouted. "He was unconscious when I got there."

"But you know who did."

Smokey leaned forward and placed his hands on the table. "I don't care what those old folks tell you. I heard the fire alarm, went in, and found the guy on the floor. Those folks saw a black kid and immediately thought I did it. I was actually trying to help that dude, who was black by the way, and those old people. But no. I'm a black kid so I'm the bad guy."

Cat stood up. "Wait here." Cat walked out of the interview room. Smokey leaned back in his chair and crossed his arms. After a few minutes, he got up and started pacing around the room. A few more minutes passed, and Smokey was still alone in the room. He started mumbling, talking to himself. More time passed. Smokey stopped and looked into the camera. "What's happening? Why am I here? Somebody talk to me. Quit playing games and talk to me."

Stanford entered the room. "Quit screaming kid."

"I'm a black kid being held prisoner for no reason," Smokey yelled. "You have no right to hold me. I haven't done anything. Just because I'm black. . ."

Stanford motioned for Smokey to sit down. "Shut up. "I'm tired of you playing the race card for everything that goes wrong in your life.

You're here because of what you've done, not because of the color of your skin. Last night, three individuals entered Comfort Cottages, the same assisted care facility we visited last week. One of the people there saw you and identified you as one of those individuals."

"I already admitted I was there," Smokey stated. "I heard the fire alarm, and I went in there to help. I saw some guy on the floor. Those old people saw me and thought I had killed him. But I had nothing to do with it. Someone else knocked the dude unconscious."

"Really?" Stanford asked. "And just what were you doing in that neighborhood that late at night? Why were you there?"

"I couldn't sleep, so I went for a walk."

"Strange place for you to be walking. First, you're hanging out in a parking lot, then you go in and a witness sees you leave that assisted-care facility with two other people."

"Some old lady sees me, and she says I ran out of the building with two other guys, and you believe her?"

"How did you know the witness was a woman?"

"Just a guess."

Stanford stood up and leaned against a wall. "You went there with two other guys. Somehow you got separated. But all three of you were involved." Stanford stood up from the wall. "Oh, by the way, we have a second witness."

Smokey gave Stanford a laugh. "Big deal. So, there's a second, or a third, or maybe even a fourth or a fifth person who saw me at the place. A lot of people saw me."

"No," Stanford said. "This witness said you were after a specific person who lives at the facility. This person said you were trying to kidnap him, who was the same person who you met there last week."

"What are you talking about?"

"Remember, we took you up there and a man identified you."

"Yeah, I remember," Smokey shouted. "And that guy said I wasn't the person you were looking for. So, why would I go back to that place? That guy said I was innocent."

Stanford scoffed. "He said you didn't kill Denise Linden. But you know he saw the killer. You were there to point him out to others. They were there to kidnap him and kill him. And you know who they are."

"You're crazy."

Stanford walked over to the door. "No, I'm not. You're the crazy one, the fool, to think that these people are going to let you go. You know too much. You can put them all in prison. Now if they killed Denise, what do you think they're going to do you."

CHAPTER TWENTY-SIX
(day eight)

Once again Smokey was left in an empty room. He sat quietly for a while before getting up and pacing around. He started shouting. An officer came in and told him to quiet down. Smokey sat down, drumming his fingers on the table in the room. He leaned back. After a while, he fell asleep. Several hours later, Detective Cat Diaz came into the room, and shook Smokey awake.

"Here, have some coffee," Cat Diaz said placing a Styrofoam cup on the table.

Smokey yawned and stretched. "What time is it?"

"Time to get up."

Smokey grabbed the coffee. "Do I get breakfast? Is this all you're going to give me?"

"I'll get you a sandwich when we get to the courthouse."

"Courthouse," Smokey yelled as he jumped up. "What's with the courthouse? You can't take me to the courthouse. I haven't done anything. I want a lawyer, and I want one right now."

"My goodness," Cat teased. "First you want breakfast and now you want a lawyer."

"What I want is to know what's going on," Smokey demanded. "Just because I'm black, you drag me in here, keep me here for hours, and now you're taking me to the courthouse so that you can throw me in jail. No way. Get me a lawyer."

"Okay," Cat said. "You'll get one when we get to the courthouse."

∞∞∞∞∞∞

Judge David McGarvey was sixty years old and spent almost half of his life on the bench overseeing family court. There were days when he hated his job. He didn't object to removing children from homes where the parents were abusive, negligent, or strung out on drugs. What he hated was having to deal with such individuals. But this case was different. The teenager was in the care of a loving grandmother, who was in ill health and this kid was her caregiver. The judge looked at Smokey and examined the police report.

"It says here that you are person of interest in a police investigation," the judge stated.

"It's a lie," Smokey yelled. "They picked me up because I'm a black man and I was in the neighborhood."

The judge motioned for Stanford to come forward. He leaned over to talk to Stanford. "Please tell me exactly why this kid is a person of interest. Is he suspected of committing a crime?"

Stanford shook his head. "No, your honor. Last week there was a homicide and Smokey, I mean Samuel, here knew the victim. We have a witness who told us that he wasn't the suspect. This witness lives at an assisted living facility However, last night there was a burglary at that assisted living facility, and Samuel was there."

"How do you know this?" the judge asked.

Stanford turned to the people in the gallery and motioned for Dot to come forward. "Your honor, this is Ms. Dorothy Fletcher. She saw Samuel in the facility last night."

"Is that right?" the judge asked Dot.

"Yes, it is. Two thugs broke into the building last night. They set off the fire alarm. When I came out of my room, two guys jumped me, tied me up and blindfolded me. It took me a few minutes before I was able to get free. But when I did, I got into my wheelchair and came out into the hall and saw Freya, our night cleaning lady, spray the two thugs with something." Dot turned and pointed to Smokey. "Then I saw that young man help the thugs get away. Fortunately, Freya was able to rescue Franklin."

The judge glanced at Stanford, then Dot. "Who's Franklin?"

"He's the person the thugs came to kidnap," Dot answered.

The judge looked at Stanford. "Can you explain this?"

Stanford motioned for Dot to return to the gallery. "According to what we were told, two unknown men entered the facility, overpowered the night attendant, then pulled the fire alarm to get everyone out of their rooms. At that time, they grabbed a resident, a Mr. Franklin Bolen, who witnessed the murder of a young lady several nights earlier. Samuel said he heard the fire alarm and went into the building to help the people."

Judge McGarvey leaned back in his chair and stared at Smokey.

"What?" screamed Smokey. "I went in to help. I should be given a medal for risking my life to these people."

"Nonsense," the judge replied before sighing. "What am I going to do with you? From this report, you are guilty of trespassing."

"But I haven't done anything," Smokey asserted.

Dot maneuvered her wheelchair next to Melissa. They started whispering to each other. The conversation became animated. Brenda joined the debate. The three of them moved the discussion to include Jennifer, who shook her head. Whatever they had in mind, it was evident that Jennifer was against it.

After a few minutes Judge McGarvey pounded his gavel. "Ladies. What is the issue?"

Melissa stood up and moved forward. "I was there last night when this young man came into our building. When I first saw him, he was over Leroy, our night attendant. At first, I thought he had hit Leroy, but he was really trying to help him. Of course, several of us started to panic and he ran off. But we didn't see him with anyone else. It's possible he saw two people who needed help and he helped them."

"That's right," Smokey shouted. "I was just helping some people in trouble."

"Really," the judge said with disbelief in his voice.

Jennifer went up to Melissa and was soon joined by Dot and Brenda. Jennifer was heard saying "no" repeatedly. Melissa moved next to Jennifer and from the gestures of the four women, it seemed Melissa, Dot, and Brenda disagreed with Jennifer. The judge allowed the discussion to continue for several minutes before he pounded his gavel again.

"Ladies," the judge shouted. "What is the issue?"

Jennifer left the group and stepped forward of the gallery. "Brenda, Melissa, and Dot suggested that this young man be assigned community service with us. We do have several odd jobs he could do."

"That's right," Dot added.

Jennifer glared at Dot.

"I take it you are not in agreement with this idea," the judge stated. "May I ask why not?"

"Because I'm black," Smokey shouted. "If I were white, there wouldn't be a problem."

"No, that's not it," Jennifer shouted back. "It's because the two times you have been to Comfort Cottages, it was because of crimes. First there was that poor woman being murdered and the second time was the break-in."

"But both times, he was innocent," Brenda added.

"That true," Jennifer said while glancing over her shoulder. She turned to face the judge. "While my concern is for the safety and welfare of our residents, Smokey, I mean Samual, does seem to need a break. He really hasn't done anything wrong."

"What we have is a charge of trespass, and community service seems fair," Judge McGarvey said as he looked at Smokey. "I'm sentencing you to 100 hours of community service at this facility."

Jennifer took a deep breath as she looked over her shoulder at Brenda and Dot. "Thank you, your honor," Jennifer replied with frustration in her voice.

Judge McGarvey snickered. "You know, I failed to ask just who you are."

"I'm Jennifer Stebbins. I'm also the manager of Comfort Cottages, an assisted living facility. The people with me are residents of the facility."

Judge McGarvey pointed his gavel at Jennifer. "From what Detective Stanford tells me, this may place your resident in danger."

"We're already in danger," Melissa answered. "Someone tried to kidnap one of our residents. Whether this young man stays with us or not is irrelevant. The danger still exists and remains the same."

The judge nodded that he agreed with Melissa's statement. He looked at Jennifer. "Do you think you can take care of and control a seventeen-year-old boy?"

"We can," Brenda answered. "It's not just Jennifer, but all of the residents."

"And what if he runs off, or simply refuses to do what you tell him to do?" the judge asked.

"What would the court do in that case?" Jennifer responded.

"Good point," Judge McGarvey answered. He motioned for Smokey to come forward. "Do you understand that you have two choices? One, I can place you in a juvenile facility. Or I can let you work for these folks. But, and I mean a very big but, you better be on your best behavior. That means you do what they tell you to do. No arguments. No ifs, ands, or buts. The choice is yours. Which is it?"

"You mean I've got to do whatever they want?" Smokey objected. "That's slavery."

"We're not going to beat you," Jennifer replied. "You will be expected to help out, go to school, and behave yourself. And remember, this is temporary, only until you complete your community service."

Smokey glared at Jennifer, who remained staring at Smokey. After a few minutes, he agreed to go with her. Neither one of them was happy with the arrangement

CHAPTER TWENTY-SEVEN

Haj was drinking coffee in his usual booth at the diner. JJ and Theo entered the diner and immediately approached Haj. Haj signaled for the waitress to bring his guests some coffee. He waited until the waitress left before speaking.

"Thanks for the coffee," Theo said.

Haj made a slight motion with his coffee to acknowledge Theo's appreciation. "Heard you botched the job."

"Wasn't our fault," JJ stated. "We had the guy and was on our way out when we ran into some cleaning lady. She almost blinded us by spraying something in our eyes. That's when she grabbed the guy and dragged him away. We would have gone after them, but Smokey came up and told us the cops were coming. So, we hightailed it out of there."

"Yeah, I heard about what happened. Did you know that Smokey got picked up by the police?"

"No, man," Theo answered. "Did he talk?"

"Who knows?" Haj replied. "But they took him to court. I heard He got community service."

"How do know that?" Theo asked.

"I have my sources," Haj answered.

"But did he talk?" JJ demanded.

"Who knows and who cares," Haj responded. "But I do need you to find Smokey."

"You want us to off him," Theo said jokingly. "Not a problem"

"Yes, it is a problem," Haj replied. "He has something I need."

"So, what do you want us to do?" JJ asked.

Haj took a sip from his coffee. "Smokey was friends with Denise Linden. You remember her?"

JJ nodded. "Yeah, we remember her."

"She had a book, a green notebook. I need that notebook."

JJ grinned. "Why? What's so important about it?"

Haj leaned forward and glared at JJ. "What's in the notebook is none of your business. It's a green notebook, a kind of ledger."

Theo pointed his coffee toward Haj. "So, what does this book have to do with Smokey?

"What I need you to do," Haj explained. "Is find Smokey and see if he knows where this notebook is. He was friends with Denise. She probably gave it to him, or he knows where it is. I don't care what you do to him but find that notebook before the cops find it."

"What about Smokey?" JJ asked.

"I told you before. I don't care what happens to him. But I do have a question for you two."

JJ and Theo squirmed in their seats. "Sure," said JJ.

"Can anyone identify either of you from that mess you pulled last night?"

"Not really," Theo answered. "We tied up one old lady, so she didn't get a good look at us. The old man didn't know what was happening, so he's no problem."

"What about the cleaning lady who sprayed you with whatever?" Haj asked.

JJ looked at Theo. "She would have seen us, but I doubt she got that good of a look at us. But don't worry. We'll take care of her."

"See that you do," Haj commanded. "It's bad enough there is one witness up there already."

CHAPTER TWENTY-EIGHT

"Meals are served at specific times," Brenda explained "Breakfast is from seven to nine. Lunch is from twelve to two, and dinner from six to eight. But there are snacks out all day. However, mealtimes don't count toward your community service."

"I know. I heard what the judge said," Smokey snidely replied. "I was there."

Breanda reached up and gave Smokey a small slap on his head. "Then remember this. If you want to be treated with courtesy and respect, then you will treat everyone with courtesy and respect."

Smokey rubbed his head. "Yes, ma'am," he softly said.

Brenda crossed her arms. "How do you treat your grandmother?"

"What do you mean?"

"I mean how do you treat her? Do show her courtesy? Do you show her respect and love?"

"Of course," Smokey answered as he sat down in one of the chairs in the dining room. "My dad abandoned us and after mother died, she took me in. One thing she always made sure of was I knew she loved me. We don't have much. But she made sure I was loved. She would sacrifice anything to take care of me."

"She sounds like a very special person."

"She is," Smokey acknowledged.

Brenda pulled out a chair and sat down facing Smokey. "So, what do you want to do?"

"What do you mean?"

"Again, with what do I mean? Do you want to make her proud of you? Do you want to help her? Do you want to take care of her?"

Smokey glared at Brenda. "Are you kidding? I would give my right arm to take care of her."

Brenda reached out and placed her hand on Smokey's. "Then let us help you so that you can help her. We're not your enemy."

"Yeah, what can you do?'

"Don't know," Brenda replied. "But I do know that there are lot of us who wish to help."

∞∞∞∞∞

After Brenda left, Smokey spent most of the day doing yard work, avoiding contact with anyone in the facility, although he saw several residents at the windows watching him. His hunger forced him to go to the dining room. He cautiously entered the dining room, stopping a few feet from the serving line.

"You need to make a decision," a woman behind him said.

Smokey turned to see an elderly woman dressed in ruffled, blue blouse and dark blue trousers. "Do I know you?" Smokey said with antagonism in his voice.

"The name is Melissa Kelsey. So, what did you and your friends want with Franklin?"

"Franklin?"

"He's the gentleman who you met the first time you were here. He's the one who said you were innocent and didn't kill that girl."

"Her name is Denise, Denise Linden. And she was a friend of mine."

"I'm sorry. I didn't mean any offense."

"That's okay," Smokey said. "Can you tell me what I need to do to get dinner?"

Melissa smiled and stepped in front of Smokey. "You just grab a tray, put your plate and flatware on it. As you go down the line, take what you want. Just remember there are others here so don't be too greedy. Then you find a table. After that, get yourself a drink, napkins, dessert, anything else you need."

Smokey grabbed a tray and a plate. "What's this for dinner?"

"An old favorite, meatloaf."

"Meatloaf?"

"Yes, meatloaf. You've heard of banana bread. Well, think of it as hamburger bread. Instead of whipped cream, you get mashed potatoes and vegetables."

Smokey chuckled. "Yeah, right." He helped himself to the food at the counter. He picked up his tray and stood at the end of the serving line. "Where can I sit?" he asked.

"With me," Melissa answered. "Love to have the company."

"I thought you didn't like me."

"I like to follow the advice of Abraham Lincoln."

"What? Free the slaves."

Melissa gave Smokey a disapproving look. "No. 'The best way to destroy an enemy is to make him a friend.' Lincoln believed that, especially after the Civil War."

"So, you're trying to make me a friend so that I won't be an enemy."

Melissa set her tray on a table and motioned for Smokey to join her. "I have a choice. I can be angry with you and dislike you, or I can try to get to know you and possibly come to like you. I've chosen the latter. Whether we become friends or not depends on you and how you behave. I'm just trying to make it easier for you. There are people here who care about what happens to you."

Smokey shyly sat down. "Thanks."

"Don't get many people caring about you, do you?"

"Just my grandma."

Melissa sat down and pointed to the drink station. "Then make yourself useful. Go get us a couple of ice teas, then tell me about your grandmother. I want to hear all about her."

CHAPTER TWENTY-NINE

Being a waitress at Barnyard Barbecue wasn't that great of a job. But Valerie knew once she completed her college degree, she would kiss this job goodbye. She wouldn't have to put up with customers making unwanted advances toward her, dirty dishes, and stingy tips. Valerie brushed her hair before putting on the cowboy hat everyone at Barnyard Barbecue wore. She put her brush in the cubbyhole she used for personal belongings. There were no lockers or any way of securing belongings, so everything in the cubbyholes was of little or no real value. As she threw her brush in the cubbyhole, she found a green notebook. Under the notebook was a calendar. It took her a moment to realize it was a calendar of Jewish holidays and observations printed on a regular calendar. Valerie opened the notebook. It was in some kind of shorthand or code. It was mostly a lot of entries with numbers. It seemed to Valerie the entries could be locations and money, but she wasn't interested in trying to figure them out. However, in the notebook was a sealed envelope addressed to Smokey. Valerie realized the note was from Denise.

∞∞∞∞∞∞

William was with his grandmother, Brenda, watching Smokey and Melissa sharing dinner together. William nudged Brenda and motioned toward Melissa. "Isn't it strange for her to be so friendly with that kid? I thought she hated him."

"Maybe it's more she hated what he did, not who he is," Brenda replied. "Besides, he's here and she's going to have to deal with him. So, why not try to be friendly. Most of us are too old to hold grudges."

∞∞∞∞∞

Dot was enjoying the evening sky when Freya pulled into the parking lot. She waved to Freya as she got out of her car and started toward the building.

The increased engine noise attracted Dot's attention as a grey sedan pulled into the parking lot. The windows were heavily tinted, making it impossible to see who was in the car. The car stopped between Freya and Dot. She tried to make out the driver when the passenger window on the other side went down, all she could see was two silhouettes of people in the front seat. Dot yelped when she heard two shots ring out. The car sped off, leaving Freya on the ground bleeding. Dot pushed her wheelchair full speed to Freya.

Joseph was entering the dining room when he heard the shots. He turned to see what was happening. William rushed pass Joseph. Brenda and several others, including Melissa and Smokey, followed William. Jennifer came out of her office and saw the crowd running outside. She followed them. Jennifer and the crowd came upon Dot in her wheelchair holding Freya's hand. "She's been shot," Dot screamed out. "Somebody call 9-1-1."

Melissa pulled out her cell phone and called for help.

William grabbed Brenda. "Get me as many clean towels as you can. Quickly." He ran over to Freya. "Stay with us. Help is on the way. You're going to be all right."

Freya knew better. She had seen too many gunshot victims in Ukraine. "Not afraid," she meekly stated. "Not afraid."

Brenda ran up and handed William some towels. "I need to keep pressure on her wounds," William said. "Get everyone back. It's best they wait inside until the ambulance and police get here. Did anyone see what happened?"

"I did," Dot answered. "A grey car came rushing into the parking lot and someone shot Freya."

Jennifer took charge and started herding the residents back in the facility. For a few moments, she was making progress. Her efforts were thwarted by the arrival of two police cars and the ambulance. Immediately everyone surged forward to see what the paramedics were going to do. Fortunately, the patrol officers were able to keep the spectators out of the paramedics' way. It took them only minutes before they had Freya on a gurney and in the ambulance. The crowd surged forward as the ambulance pulled away.

A patrol sergeant arrived on the scene. Once he established the crowd was under control, he approached William. "You have quite a bit of blood on you. Can you tell me what happened?"

"Heard gunshots and ran out here to find the victim on the ground. Tried to stop the bleeding until the ambulance arrived."

"Anyone see what happened?" the sergeant asked.

"I did," Dot shouted with tears in her eyes. "A grey car pulled into the parking lot and someone shot poor Freya, for no reason."

"What kind of car?" the officer asked.

"It was a four-door car," Dot answered.

"Did it have a trunk or was the back of the car kind of square?"

"It had a trunk."

The sergeant pushed the button on his radio and broadcasted the description of the car.

Jennifer came forward and put her hands on Dot's shoulders. "Why don't you come into my office where the police officer can talk to you privately."

"But what about Freya?"

"We'll all pray for her," Brenda said. "But right now. You need to tell the police everything you know. That's the only way they will catch whoever did this."

"Come with me," Jennifer said, gently encouraging Dot to follow her.

William, along with Joseph and Brenda, started herding the residents back into the facility. Melissa remained back for a moment. She noticed Smokey was no longer here."

CHAPTER THIRTY
(day nine)

Jennifer hated starting the day with a visit to the hospital. But with Freya being shot yesterday, she had no choice. It wasn't a sense of duty that compelled her to come. It was the loyalty she felt to someone who was a part of the Comfort Cottages community. Jennifer along with Melissa and Brenda cautiously approached the nurses' station in ICU. A middle-aged nurse dressed in blue scrubs looked up from her computer. "Can I help you?"

Jennifer pulled out a HIPAA form. "I'm Jennifer Stebbins. We're here to see Freya Serban. She was shot yesterday in the parking lot of Comfort Cottages, where she works. I'm her supervisor and her emergency point of contact."

The nurse stood up and took the HIPAA from Jennifer. She spent a minute going over it. "Yes, I was informed you are her emergency point of contact. Strange she would have her employer as her emergency contact."

"She's a refugee from Ukraine," Jennifer explained. "We're sponsoring her and looking after her while she's here in the United States. The rest of her family, what's left of it, is still in Ukraine. If you wish, you may call Dr. Oscar Cowell. He's the doctor we use at Comfort Cottages, and he's familiar with our situation."

"Just give me a minute," the nurse said as she placed the HIPAA form on the counter. She picked up the phone and punched in some numbers. While Jennifer couldn't hear what was said at the other end, she knew the nurse had reached Dr. Cowell, who confirmed Jennifer was responsible for Freya. After a brief conversation, the nurse replaced the handset and returned the form to Jennifer.

"Sorry about the delay," the nurse said. "Ms. Serban is in room seven in the ICU. She's heavily sedated, so I doubt she will be awake. But I'll have Dr. Robinson, the surgeon who operated on her, come and talk to you."

Jennifer thanked the nurse before she, Brenda, and Melissa went to see Freya. They entered Freya's room to find her attached to several wires leading to a machine monitoring her vitals. Freya was asleep. Brenda walked over to her and took her hand. "I don't want to wake her up, but I do want her to know that we're here for her. I don't want her to feel alone."

Jennifer sat down in one of the two chairs in the room. "I know what you mean. She doesn't have her real family here."

"I far as I'm concerned, we are her real family," Brenda said, turning to face Jennifer. "We may not share the same blood, but no one cares more about her than we do."

Jennifer admired the loyalty and love the residents had for the people in their lives. Too often they were left in the facility by family members who were too busy to visit, forgot their birthdays, failed to include them in family events such as holiday celebrations. So, they expanded their kindness and caring to those who did visit and did play a part in their daily lives.

A small man wearing a blue shirt and striped tie entered the room. "I was informed that Ms. Jennifer Stebbins is here."

"I'm Jennifer."

"I'm Dr. Robinson. I was the one who operated on your friend. I understand you are her emergency contact."

"That's right," Jennifer said as she approached the doctor. "Freya is a refugee who works at the facility that I manage. She has no family here in the United States."

"So, we're family now," Brenda asserted.

Jennifer put her hand on Brenda's before turning to face the doctor. "Could you tell us how she's doing? Will she be all right?"

"The gunshot injuries were life-threatening. She made it through surgery just fine. We were able to remove the bullets and stop the bleeding. While she's still in critical condition, barring any complications, she should recover. But it's going to be a long recovery. She'll need special care."

"How long will she have to stay in the hospital? Jennifer asked.

The doctor took a deep breath. "If everything goes well, we may be able to release her in a week or ten days. It really depends on how well she responds to treatment."

"What treatment?" Brenda demanded.

"We want to make sure there are no complications or infections. Also, we want to make sure she can get the care she'll need after she leaves."

"We'll take care of that," Jennifer stated. "She works at Comfort Cottages, an assisted-living facility. We have a nurse on staff and access to a doctor 24 hours a day. We'll make sure she gets everything she needs."

"That's good to hear," the doctor responded. "But for now, what she really needs is rest and time to heal from the surgery. She'll probably be in intensive care for the next few days. After that, we'll see what can be done." The doctor checked Freya's chart before saying goodbye.

Leroy entered the room just as the doctor left. He stopped at the door when he saw Jennifer with Brenda and Melissa next to Freya's bed. "Hey," he said clearing his throat. "I didn't know anyone was here with her."

Melissa walked over and took Leroy's hand in hers. "So good to see you. I hope you're all right. We were so worried when we found you on the floor the other night."

"I'm okay. It was just a bump on the head. They kept me to make sure there wasn't anything serious like a blood clot in the brain. But I'm doing fine and I hope they release me today. How's Freya doing?"

"She was shot yesterday," Jennifer answered. "Someone drove up and shot her in the parking lot of the facility. We're lucky she's alive. We can only pray she recovers."

Melissa stepped into the hall and looked around before returning to Jennifer. "There's no one there."

"What do you mean?" Jennifer inquired. "Are the nurses gone?"

"No, I don't mean that. I mean there's no police protection."

Jennifer slightly tilted her head. "Police protection?"

"Yes. Police protection. Freya was shot. She was targeted. That means someone wanted to kill her. There should a police officer outside her door protecting her."

Jennifer took a moment to reflect on what Melissa said. "I see your point. There's nothing to stop whoever shot her from coming here and shooting her again. But how do we get her police protection?"

"I don't know," Melissa answered.

"Until then, I can stay with her," Leroy said. "I may not be the best defense against a killer with a gun, but I'm better than nothing. At least until you do get Freya police protection."

"Good," Melissa replied, "and I know where we can start."

CHAPTER THIRTY-ONE

Melissa insisted Jennifer accompany her to the police station. They entered the foyer that had a long bench along the wall to the right of the entrance. Above the bench were several posters giving crime prevention tips and suicide prevention. The wall opposite the entrance had a large plexiglass window with a depression at the bottom, enabling people to pass documents back and forth on the counter. The left wall had two doors, one led to the operations rooms where patrol officers conducted their business, the other led to a stairway going to the second floor where the administrative and detectives' officers were. Melissa charged the desk sergeant's window like a tiger going after fresh meat.

"I need to see the detectives handling the shooting that took place at Comfort Cottages yesterday," Melissa commanded. "It's a matter of life or death."

The desk sergeant was a fourteen-year veteran and used to citizens demanding action. He calmly put up his hands to show he understood Melissa's demand. "Okay. Could you tell me who you are? Possibly show me some identification?"

Melissa opened her purse and pulled out her driver's license. She placed in the depression for the desk sergeant. He looked at Jennifer, who took it as a sign she was to provide her identification as well, which she did. The desk sergeant took both drivers' licenses, examined them before picking up the phone. After he got off the phone, he returned Melissa's and Jennifer's drivers' licenses. The desk sergeant informed them detectives would be down in a few minutes and they should have a seat on the bench in the foyer. Jennifer and Melissa didn't have long to wait.

Stanford and Cat opened one of the doors in the foyer. Stanford nodded to Melissa. "Good to see you."

Jennifer stood up. "We just came from the hospital where Freya is. She's alone there. There's no police protection. There's nothing to keep whoever shot her to go and shoot her again."

"Isn't she in intensive care?' Cat asked. "She's being constantly monitored. There are nurses, and the hospital has security. I'm sure she's safe."

"No, she's not," Melissa insisted. "It's too easy for someone to go into her room unnoticed. The nurses are busy, and security is mostly on the first floor."

Cat and Stanford glanced at each other. She turned to face Jennifer and Melissa. "You do have some good points. But it will take us a while to get someone there to stand watch at the hospital. It might not be until tomorrow morning. We'll see what we can do."

"Thank you," Melissa replied. "But what about tonight? Will she be safe?"

Stanford raised his hand to get Melissa's attention. "I'll call the hospital and have them put a security guard outside her room until we can get a patrol officer to take over. Still, I want you both to come upstairs and look at some photographs."

∞∞∞∞∞∞

Stanford laid out two sets of photographs for Jennifer and Melissa to view. One set held photos of men who were short and thin. The other set held photos of individuals of a muscular build. JJ's photo was in the first set, and Theo's in the second.

"I want you to take a look at each set of photographs and see if you recognize anyone," Stanford explained to Melissa. "Take your time and look at them carefully."

Melissa did as she was instructed. After a few minutes, she turned to Stanford and shook her head. "I'm sorry, but I don't recognize any of them. Who are they?"

"We think maybe the people who broke into your facility were in this group," Stanford explained."

"Well, I certainly can't help you," Melissa replied. "I didn't see them. The only person who could possibly identify them is Freya."

"That's okay," Stanford assured her. "Didn't figure you could, but it was worth a try."

Jennifer stepped over to the table and stared at the photos. "I don't know if it means anything, but I recognize one of the men in the photos.

"Which one," Cat asked.

Jennifer pointed to the photo of JJ. "Him."

Cat picked up the photo. "How do know him?"

"He came in a couple of days ago asking about Comfort Cottages. He said he was looking for a place for his grandmother."

Cat picked out the photo of Theo, placing it next to one of JJ. "I don't want to alarm you, but if he came to your facility, he may have been checking it out and later burglarized the place. I do want you to remember these two individuals. It's possible they had something to do with your friend being shot and the murder of Denise Linden. She was the woman killed in the parking lot of the restaurant behind your building. If you do see them, call us immediately." Cat pulled out her business card. "My cell phone is on the card. So, any time day or night, if they show up, call." Stanford also gave the ladies his business card.

∞∞∞∞∞∞

Jennifer was tired as she and Melissa returned to Comfort Cottages. Seeing William there, helping his grandmother, Brenda, and Dot working on a jigsaw puzzle, gave Jennifer new energy. Jennifer noticed Susan was standing next to William. Melissa smiled and excused herself as she joined Joseph and Franklin watching a game show on the large screen TV in the rec room.

"Oh, I'm so glad you're back," Brenda said to Jennifer as she patted William's hand. Obviously, a signal for him to engage Jennifer in conversation.

"How is Freya?" Susan asked.

Jennifer set her bag down. "She's in critical condition. The doctor didn't say it, but I got the impression that it's touch and go at the moment. But she made it through surgery. She's in intensive care, they are keeping a close eye on her."

"What can we do?" Dot asked.

"Keep her in your prayers," Jennifer replied. "All we can do is hope for the best. Not to change the subject, but I am. William, what are you doing here?"

"There was a murder, you had a break in, and a shooting. I'm staying here until the cops catch whoever is responsible,"

Brenda again placed her hand on William's arm. "Besides, we like the company."

"And he makes us feel safe," Susan blurted out while she hugged William's arm.

William skillfully disconnected himself from Susan. "I hope you don't mind."

"Are you going to be here 24/7?" Jennifer asked. "What about your job? Don't you have to go to work?"

"Not a problem. Got some others to cover for us. Hopefully they won't have to do it for long. I asked a couple of my buddies to join me. I figured having a few extra bodies around wouldn't hurt."

Jennifer took a moment before responding. "Well, for now, I guess it would be okay. Especially since Leroy won't be back until tomorrow. Having more people around would be good. How about you and your buddies being our night watchmen? We'll set up something so you can sleep during the day. But you and your buddies are not to take any risks. I don't want anyone getting hurt trying to be a hero. If you see anything, call the police. Is that clear?"

"Got 9-1-1 on speed dial," William replied.

CHAPTER THIRTY-TWO
[day ten]

It was late afternoon and Smokey sat in his car, drumming his fingers on the steering wheel, watching people go into the funeral home. *I should go in,* he thought to himself. *Denise was my friend. Yeah, it was more of a business thing, but she always treated me right. I really should go in and pay my respects.* Smokey turned on the ignition and ran the air conditioner. He didn't want to wait out in the open in case JJ, Theo, or Haj were around. There was no reason for them to show up. They didn't know Denise; well, Haj did. But after the shooting two days ago, Smokey couldn't be sure. He hadn't seen who shot the woman at Comfort Cottages, but when he realized it was the cleaning woman who had sprayed JJ and Theo with a cleaning solution, he was fairly certain it was JJ and Theo.

Smokey looked down at his clothes. He was wearing dark trousers, a blue dress shirt with a dark blue tie. He didn't have a nice jacket to go with his outfit, but he figured it was more important for him to be there than anything else. He turned off the engine and opened the door of his car. He closed it and stood by it, rubbing his hands on his trousers. He didn't want to have sweaty palms. Even after drying his hands, he remained next to his car, trying to convince himself to go inside. That's when he saw one of Denise's coworkers approaching the funeral home.

He looked around before crossing the parking lot and walking up to the young woman. "Excuse me," Smokey said, hoping he wasn't scaring the woman. "Don't you work with Denise?"

The woman faced Smokey. "That's right. I remember you. You come by just about every week. I'm Valerie, by the way."

"That's right," Smokey replied. "Smokey. Denise and I were friends. Are you going to the funeral?" Smokey wanted to hit himself for asking such a ridiculous question.

Valerie smiled. "Yeah. Figured at least one person from work should show up."

Smokey saw a green notebook. "Hey. I think you have my notebook. I lent it to Denise, but she never gave it back to me." Before the woman could say anything, he grabbed it out from her. "Thanks for getting this back to me."

"Wait a minute," Valerie said. "Maybe it's Denise's. I mean, how do I know it's yours?"

"Tell you what. If it's mine, it's going to have a lot of numbers in it. It's an idea for an accounting system I'm trying out. Denise was going to check to see if it worked. Let's open it up and see what's inside."

Valerie was about to object, even though she knew it was supposed to go to Smokey, when her attention was drawn to a car that pulled into the parking lot and stopped suddenly. Smokey turned to see JJ and Theo getting out of their car. He took off running. JJ and Thero followed.

∞∞∞∞∞

Melissa always saw funerals as sad things. She got out of the van from Comfort Cottages, along with Brenda, Joseph, Dot, and Franklin. The van parked in front of the funeral home to let everyone out. Just as they started toward the funeral home, Smokey ran pass them. He was followed by two white guys, one of them slender and short, the other was big and muscular.

"I think I know that kid," Franklin said as he followed the group. Franklin disappeared around the corner of the building.

"For an old fart, he can certainly move when he wants to," Joseph said with a giggle.

"But he's right," Melissa said. "That's Smokey. He disappeared when Freya was shot. And I wouldn't be surprised if the two chasing that kid were the ones who did it and tried to grab Franklin. Come on. Let's get Franklin before he gets himself into trouble."

Melissa, Brenda, and Joseph went around the building hunting for Franklin. Dot remained in her wheelchair, waiting by the van. After a few minutes, Joseph, Melissa, and Brenda found Franklin standing by several bushes. He was holding a green notebook.

"What have you got there, Franklin?" Melissa asked as she led the group back to the van and Dot.

"A book," answered Franklin. "I found it over there in the bushes."

"We can see that," Joseph said while twirling his finger next to his head.

Brenda jabbed Joseph in the ribs. "Stop that. He's not crazy."

When they got to the van and rejoined Dot, Melissa stepped up to Franklin. "May I see the book?" Franklin handed the notebook to her. She opened it and examined several pages. "At first glance, I would say it's some kind of ledger. But it doesn't make sense to me."

"Let me see it," Dot commanded. "I used to do some bookkeeping. Maybe I can figure it out."

Melissa handed the notebook to Dot, who examined several pages. "It's a ledger all right. But it's in some kind of shorthand or code."

Brenda clapped her hands together. "Well Dot, you love puzzles. I bet you can figure it out. It might take some time, and we have plenty of that. You should keep the book until you can figure it out and tell us what it means."

"Sounds like an excellent idea," Melissa stated in agreement. "However, right now, we should get inside and pay our respects to the woman whose funeral we are attending."

Upon entering the sanctuary, there was a small crowd, which made Melissa pleased that all five of them decided to attend. Melissa and the others realized it was a Jewish service when they saw the Star of David and the men wearing yarmulkas.

"Do you know who her family is?" Brenda asked.

Melissa gave Brenda a disappointing look. "We're all strangers here. The only person who ever saw the deceased is Franklin, and it's a fifty-fifty chance he'll remember her."

"Looks like it's a closed coffin affair anyway," Dot commented. "Makes sense. I heard she was beaten to death. Better for everyone to remember as she was."

"Hey, there's someone we know," Joseph said as he pointed to a young woman. "That's the waitress we talked to at Barnyard Barbecue."

"Well, then let's say hello," Melissa said, encouraging the others to follow her.

As the group approached the young woman, Melissa held out her hand. "How nice to see you again," she said. "I do hope you remember us. We talked to you about your friend the other day when we were at your restaurant."

The young woman shook Melissa's hand. "Yes, I remember you."

"I'm sorry for the loss of your friend," said Melissa. "Also, forgive me, but I've forgotten your name."

"It's Valerie Tungson."

"Well, Valerie. Could you point out your friend's family so that we may pay our respects."

Valerie pointed to a woman wearing a black dress and a red scarf. Next to her was a man with thinning hair and another young woman.

"Thank you," Melissa replied. "May I ask if you were close to the deceased?"

"No, not really. I just think someone from work should be here. I really don't know what to say to them. I just worked with Denise. It's not like we were friends or anything."

"That's not what's important," Melissa said placing her hand on Valerie's arm. "It shows that the people where she worked thought enough of her to pay their respects to her and her family."

Valerie thanked Melissa for her words of encouragement. Melissa and the others took seats toward the back of the room. The service was short and afterwards they all made it a point to pay their respects to the family. They were invited to the family's home for refreshments, but Melissa encouraged the others in the group to decline. She knew the what the family really needed was time to deal with their grief, something that many found was best done alone. They returned to the facility's van for the ride back to Comfort Cottages. The five of them talked about how glad they made the effort to attend. While Franklin, Joseph, Brenda, and Melissa experienced some feelings of grief over the tragic events that took Denise Linden's life; Dot's thoughts were focused on the green notebook she had in her bag.

CHAPTER THIRTY-THREE

William was sitting in a rocking chair under the awning over the front entrance to Comfort Cottages. Jennifer parked her car and walked up to William. "Look like you're beginning to enjoy the lifestyle around here."

"It is kind of relaxing. Time to sit, watch TV, read a book, admire the flowers in the garden."

Jennifer turned around and looked at the small grassy area in the front of the building. "The only flowers we have here are weeds. Which reminds me, I need to get someone out here to cut the lawn."

"If need be, one of us can do it," William replied. "Us firefighters aren't afraid of work."

"I'll remember that," Jennifer said as she sat in a rocking chair next to William. "So, are you out here to watch the grass grow, or is this your post from which you will protect us?"

William chuckled. "I'm just waiting for my grandmother to get back from that funeral she and her friends are attending. You know, the one for the woman that was killed."

Jennifer nodded. "Yes, I remember. It's kind of nice of them to attend. I'm sure the family appreciates it."

"Well, not to change the subject. . ."

"But you are."

William chuckled again. "Yeah, I am. Where have you been?"

"I went back to the hospital to check on Freya."

"How's she doing?"

"Better, but she's still in intensive care. But she did regain consciousness, which is a good sign. I'm hoping she doesn't have to stay there too much longer. But the good news is there is a police officer outside her door. We don't have to worry about anyone going into her room and harming her. And Leroy was released. He'll be back to work this evening."

"Has she told the police anything?"

Jennifer shook her head. "She regained consciousness. She's kind of out of it. When she is awake, she seems frightened. I told the nurse to call me when she wakes up. I think seeing a familiar face will calm her down."

"I'm sure Grandma and her friends will be glad to visit her while she's in the hospital."

Jennifer touched William's arm. It sent a surge of energy through him. Jennifer pointed to the facility's van as it pulled into the parking lot.

"Here comes your grandmother now."

Melissa was the first one off the bus, followed by Brenda and Joseph. Franklin waited until the driver lowered Dot in her wheelchair to the ground before he stepped off the van.

"How was the funeral?" William asked as the group approached the building entrance.

"I found a book," Franklin proudly stated. "It was green."

Brenda reached over and patted Franklin on the shoulder. "Yes, you did. And you gave it to Dot. She has it now. Later we'll all sit down and look at it together."

"I know that," Franklin shouted. "I'm not a fool. But I found the book."

"What kind of book was it?" Jennifer asked.

"We really don't know," Dot replied. "It looks like a ledger, but it's hard to understand. There's a column with numbers that could be dates, and another column is numbers which could be money. But the other columns don't make sense. But I will figure it out. You can depend on me."

"Not that really matters," Melissa commented. "We don't know where it came from or who it belongs to. Even if we do figure it out, it's useless unless we know whose book it is."

"That's true," William stated. "Still, if you can figure out what it says, that might lead you to whose book it is."

Dot pulled the green notebook out of her bag. "I'll figure it out. I'm really good at puzzles, and this isn't anything more than a puzzle. Trust me. I'll figure it out."

∞∞∞∞∞∞

Smokey watched from the second floor of an abandoned building. JJ and Theo were searching for him, but each step they took led them farther from him. Smokey waited until they were out of sight before coming down. He headed back to the funeral home, hoping to get there before JJ and Theo. He needed to get the green notebook.

CHAPTER THIRTY-FOUR

Valerie greeted Stanford and Cat as they entered Barnyard Barbecue. She handed them menus and left. A minute later she returned with glasses of water. "Would you like something to drink?" she asked.

"Coffee and what kind of pie do you have?" Stanford responded.

"We have cherry, apple, peach, and pecan. I recommend the apple. It's fresh and really good."

"Sounds good," Cat said. "We'll both take coffee and some apple pie."

"How do you know I want apple?" Stanford asked.

"Then, what kind do you want?" Cat teased.

"Apple," Stanford replied.

"Sure thing," Valerie said as she picked up the menus. "Are you sure you don't want dinner?"

"No thanks," Cat answered.

"By the way, I'm glad you guys came in."

"Why's that?" said Cat.

"Well, when you were in here last time, you asked about Denise's friend."

"Samuel Corden, also known as Smokey," Stanford said after glancing at Cat.

"Yeah," Valerie affirmed. "I saw him this afternoon."

"Where?" Stanford asked.

"At Denise's funeral. I thought at least one of us should be there."

"That's very thoughtful of you dear," Cat said. "What about Samuel?"

"Oh, yeah. Well, he was there. He grabbed a green notebook Denise left for him. Then, he took off running. Two guys started chasing him. Then some old people ran after them."

"Old people?" said Stanford. "Were they from the place behind here?"

"Yeah, they were there at the funeral too. They were very nice."

Cat stood up. "We're going to have to skip the coffee and pie."

∞∞∞∞∞∞

Jennifer was standing with William inside the front entrance when William noticed Stanford and Cat as they pulled into the parking lot of Comfort Cottages. "Wonder what they want?" William said to Jennifer.

Jennifer clasped her hands together. "I hope it isn't bad news about Freya?"

"Nah," William responded. "The hospital would have called. They wouldn't have sent the police."

"Evening," said Cat as she and Stanford entered the assisted living facility. "How is everyone doing?"

"We're fine," a worried Jennifer answered. "Is this about Freya? Is she all right? Has something happened to her?"

"No, no," Cat answered. "Your friend is fine. She's still at the hospital and we have security on her. We're here to talk about Samuel Corden, AKA Smokey. We understand some of your residents may have seen him today at Denise Linden's funeral."

"Well, Melissa and several others did go to her funeral. But you will have to ask them if they saw Smokey."

"Can you get them?" Stanford asked.

"Follow me," Jennifer said, turning to lead the detectives to the rec room. The detectives, with William and Jennifer, found Melissa reading a book.

"Melissa," Jennifer said, tapping Melissa on her shoulder. "Detectives Agusta and Diaz would like to talk to you. They said you saw Smokey at the funeral."

Melissa stood up to face the detectives, "That's right. We saw him when we got off the bus at the funeral home. We saw him run pass us. There were two guys running after him. Before we knew it, Franklin ran after them. We, of course, ran after Franklin. Once we caught up with Franklin, we all went into the funeral home. It was a lovely service. I'm glad we went. It was shame there weren't more people attending the service."

"What about Smokey?" Stanford asked. "Was he at the funeral?"

"No. We saw him for only a moment."

"Isn't he here?" asked Cat. "I thought he was placed here doing community service."

Melissa nodded. "He was here. But after Freya was shot, he ran off."

Stanford huffed and placed his hands on his hips. "Why didn't you notify us?"

Melissa held up her head. "I was unaware we were to notify you. However, we did notify the courts."

"But you saw him today," Stanford affirmed. "You said he was running from a couple of guys. Can you describe them?"

Melissa shook her head. "Not really. One of them was big, kind of like a football player. The other guy was smaller."

Cat went up to Melissa and placed her hand on her arm. "Could they have been the same ones who broke in here a couple of nights ago?"

Melissa took a breath. "It's possible."

"Is there anything more you can tell me about the two men chasing Smokey?" Stanford asked.

"Sorry, I'm afraid not."

∞∞∞∞∞

Melissa waited until Jennifer and William left with the detectives. She looked at her watch. She turned and walked down the hall. She stopped and knocked gently on the door to Dot's room. "Come in," a voice replied from behind the door. Melissa opened the door and entered the room.

"Well, welcome," Dot said as she maneuvered her chair to face Melissa. "What brings you here?"

"Two detectives were just here. They were asking about Smokey. Someone told them we saw him at the funeral this afternoon."

"Did you tell them about the notebook?"

Melissa shook her head. "No, but I'm beginning to think that maybe that notebook may be important. Have you figured it out yet?"

"Not yet," Dot answered. "But I'm sure you're right about it being important. It's awfully complicated for a simple ledger." Dot held up the notebook. "This ledger has secrets. And I believe it's those secrets that got the poor girl killed."

CHAPTER THIRTY-FIVE
(day eleven)

Stanford was standing in his office, examining the police records for Joseph Jacobs, aka JJ, and for Theo Karlow. Both individuals were in separate interviews rooms. Cat sat at her desk drinking coffee, waiting for Stanford.

"What do you want to do?" she asked.

"I want to go home, get a cold beer, and watch TV, providing my wife will let me. But since we have these two here, guess we should talk to them."

Cat grinned. "You know they won't tell us anything. Look at their records. They've been suspected of several homicides. Both of them have been brought in before. They're more afraid of cockroaches than they are us."

"I know," Stanford said. "Still, I want them to know we're watching them. Maybe it will cause them to slip up."

"Okay," Cat said as she stood up. "Which one do you want?"

Stanford held up one of the files. "I'll take Joseph. You can have Theo."

∞∞∞∞∞∞

Stanford entered the interview room. Before he could sit down, JJ shouted, "I want a lawyer."

Stanford ignored the demand and sat down. "You know what I want? I'll tell you. I want a cold beer and maybe some barbecued ribs. I haven't had ribs in a long time."

"Who cares what you want old man," JJ shouted.

Stanford held up his hands. "Please, quit yelling. I'm right here. Just talk to me. There's no need to shout."

JJ leaned forward and stated in a low voice full of authority. "I want a lawyer."

"That's much better. Now about that lawyer. Don't worry. We'll get you one. Just be patient."

"Then we don't have anything to talk about."

"Not true," Stanford said as he opened JJ's police record.

"Not going to work," JJ asserted. "I was in the army. I was trained to withstand interrogations."

Stanford giggled. "You were a clerk who served three years at Fort Meade in Maryland and two tours in Iraq, *as a clerk*. Your greatest accomplishment was getting an honorable discharge."

"Yeah, at least I served."

"And thank you for your service, no matter how limited it was." Stanford knew the comment was uncalled for, but he wanted to take JJ down a peg or two. "Now, you asked for a lawyer. That's your right. But what is strange to me is you didn't ask why we brought you in. Don't you want to know why you're here?"

"Okay. Tell me."

Stanford waved a finger at JJ. "Now. Now. Be nice. As you know, there was a break-in at Comfort Cottages a couple of nights ago. Two individuals, who seem to match your description along with that of your friend, were seen there. The next day, two individuals shot a cleaning woman who works there."

"What's that got to do with us? We didn't do it. We were nowhere near that old folks' home."

Stanford smiled. "I never said what kind of facility Comfort Cottages was. How did you know it was an old folks' home."

JJ glared at Stanford. "Where's my lawyer."

∞∞∞∞∞∞

Cat walked into the interview room and closed the door. She stood there for a moment, looking at Theo. He stared back, silent. She could see he was unsure of the situation. "Good morning," Cat said as she approached Theo.

"Yeah. Hello and all that. What do you want?"

Cat pulled out a chair and sat down. "Well, since you're here, I'd like to talk to you about a few things."

Theo pushed his chair back and held up palms. "No way. I know better than to talk to the cops without a lawyer. You're not pinning anything on me. I ain't done nothing."

"The correct phrase is 'I haven't done anything.' Didn't you learn grammar in school?"

"Listen bitch. I didn't come here for a grammar lesson."

Cat placed her elbows on the table and motioned for Theo to come closer. He scooted his chair forward. She motioned for him to still come closer. He leaned forward. Cat grabbed Theo's nose and pulled it to her. "You call me a bitch one more time, and I will remove body parts and pin them to my bulletin board." She let go, pushing Theo back.

"That hurt."

"Good," said Cat. "Now you'll know to show me some courtesy and respect."

Theo rubbed his nose. "Why am I here? You can't keep me here."

Cat leaned back in her chair. "Maybe I want to get your opinion on the war in Ukraine or about the boarder crises in Texas and Arizona."

"They both suck," Theo answered vehemently.

"Then let's talk about what happened a couple of nights ago at Comfort Cottages."

"No way," Theo shouted. "We had nothing to do with that break-in."

Cat grinned. "What about the shooting that took place there the next day."

"We…" Theo stopped. He leaned back. "What shooting? We weren't there."

"All right. Then explain why you were seen chasing Samuel Corden at a funeral home yesterday?"

"Who's this Samuel Corden?'

"You know him as Smokey."

"Who said we chased Smokey?"

"Some people saw you there."

"What? Some old people? They need glasses to find their way to the bathroom."

"Never said they were old people," Cat commented.

"That's it," Theo yelled. "I want a lawyer. Get me one, and I mean now."

Cat stood up and walked to the door before turning to face Theo. "Sit tight. I'll be back." She left before Theo could respond.

* * * * *

Haj was not known for his patience. Sitting at his usual place in the diner, he kept playing with the flatware on the table. His coffee cup was empty, but he didn't want a refill. What he wanted was to know where JJ and Theo were. He wanted to know where Smokey was. Most of all, he wanted to know where that green notebook was. He looked at his cell phone. He placed another call to JJ. It went to voice mail. Haj didn't leave a message. He didn't need to. JJ and Theo entered the diner.

"Where have you two been?" Haj demanded.

"Hey!" JJ shouted. "Don't give us any crap. We spent the morning at the police station."

"Lower your voice," Haj said while motioning with his chin that they were attracting attention. "What happened? Why did the police bring you in?"

"They were questioning us about stuff," Theo answered.

Before Haj could say anything, JJ interrupted. "They brought us in for questioning about what happened at that old folks' home. But they've got nothing. They kept us there, but after a while, they let us go. Nothing to worry about."

"They also asked us about the woman that was shot there," Theo added.

"What woman?" Haj demanded. "What shooting?"

JJ fidgeted in his seat. "When we broke into the place, a cleaning woman sprayed us with something. We figured she got a good look at us. So, we went back the next day and killed her. Can't have any witnesses."

"Can't have any witnesses," Haj hissed. "Then how did the cops know it was you who shot her? Someone saw you."

"Not possible," JJ insisted. "We used a stolen car for the job. It had tinted windows. No one saw anything."

"And what about the old man?" Haj asked. "Have you taken care of him?"

"Not yet," JJ answered.

"Let me get this straight," Haj said. "You haven't taken out the old man, who you tried to kidnap. You shot the only witness who saw you that night. But the police seem to know it was you two who did these things. So, who told them?"

"It had to be Smokey," JJ responded.

"That's right. It had to be Smokey," said Theo.

Haj took a deep breath and shook his head. "What about the green notebook I asked you to find?"

Theo shrugged his shoulders. "Maybe Smokey has it."

Haj leaned forward and pointed his fingers at JJ and Theo. "Then you two find Smokey and get that notebook. Then make sure that old man who saw Denise killed and Smokey can no longer talk."

CHAPTER THIRTY-SIX

Melissa entered the dining room. William was leaning on the counter where the coffee urn and breakfast pastries were. Standing in front of him was Jennifer with a cup in her hand. She tried to get around William for some coffee. He extended his arms to block her. They were both smiling, enjoying the game.

"Sorry to interrupt," Melissa said as she approached the couple. "But Jennifer is going to need her coffee, and so do I."

William stepped aside and waved his arm to grant the ladies access to their morning beverage.

"Thank you," Melissa acknowledged. She looked at Jennifer. "Better drink up and I suggest grabbing a muffin or two. I'm going to need your help today, if you don't mind."

Jennifer and William stared at Melissa. "Of course not. What can I do for you?" Jennifer asked.

Melissa filled a cup with coffee before turning and looking around, ensuring no one else was listening. "Yesterday we saw Smokey at the funeral for the poor girl that was murdered. However, when we saw him, he was running from two others. I wouldn't be surprised to find out they were the two who broke in here last week. Whether they were or not, it's obvious that Smokey is in trouble. I think we should try to find him and see what we can do to help."

"That's commendable," William said. "But the police are better equipped to help him. I don't mean to be rude, but what can you or anyone here do to protect him?"

Mellisa took a sip of her coffee. She maneuvered around William to take a muffin. "Smokey lives with his grandmother who is not in the best of health. Perhaps knowing there are others who care about him and will provide the guidance he needs to handle the situation may lead to a solution. Besides, I get the feeling the last place Smokey will go for help or protection is the police."

Jennifer looked at William before turning her attention to Melissa. "Still, there is very little we can do."

"We told the court that we would look after Smokey while he did his community service here at Comfort Cottages," Melissa stated. "To be honest, I don't know what we can do, but I feel we should at least try to help him. We just might be the ones who can keep him out of trouble. I would hate to think he ends up in jail when we could have done something." Melissa took a deep breath. "Please, help me find him. Let's see if we can't help."

William nodded in agreement. "Okay, but I'm coming with you. Do you have any idea on how to find him?"

Melissa raised her chin. "Of course. I wouldn't have asked if I didn't have some place to start. We should visit his grandmother."

∞∞∞∞∞∞

The house was a modest two-story home with a wooden yawning covering a large front porch. Melissa led Jennifer and William to the front door. She rang the doorbell. They heard sounds of motion from inside the house, then a voice asking who was there.

"I'm Melissa Kelsey. I'm here with Jennifer Stebbins and William Barlow. We're from Comfort Cottages where your grandson does some work for us.

The front door opened, as elderly woman with a walker stood on the other side of the screen door. Her gray hair framed her brown, wrinkled face. Dressed in a robe over a nightgown and in slippers, she examined the three, white people at her door. "What can I do for you folks?" she asked with apprehension in her voice.

Jennifer placed her hand on her chest. "We're looking for Ms. Teresa Simpson, the grandmother of Smokey, I mean Samuel. He does some work for us and we haven't seen him for a couple of days. We're a bit worried about him."

"I'm Samual's grandmother. But how can I help you? He's a grown boy. Takes care of himself. What can you do for him?"

William cleared his throat, but Jennifer put up her hand to silence him. "Yesterday, there was a funeral for a friend of his." Jennifer motioned toward Melissa. "Several of our residents, including Melissa, saw two men chasing Smokey. We're afraid he may be in trouble. We want to help him. If you know where he might be, maybe you could have him get in touch with us."

The elderly woman stared at Jennifer, Melissa, and William. She then looked around them to see if anyone else was in the street. "You seem like nice people, but I don't know you. And I've dealt with you social services people before. You get our hopes up and then leave us with nothing but promises and empty air. I thank you for your concern, but Samual and I will take care of ourselves."

"I understand your reservations," Jennifer replied. She pulled out a business card. "Please take my card. Let Smokey know we care about him and we will help him. We would really like for him to call us." Jennifer slipped her card in between the screen door and the door frame.

"May I say something," Melissa insisted. "Ms. Simpson, you're right not to trust us, and I can't blame you. But we know you are in poor health. And we really do want to help Smokey. Please have him call us. Also, if you need anything, give us a call. I'm a resident of an assisted-living facility, so I know how hard it is to get the help you need. We're here if you need us."

Simpson bowed her head and took a step back. "I thank you for your concern. You all take care." She closed the door.

CHAPTER THIRTY-SEVEN

Smokey wiped his hands on the front of his pants. He held up his arm and sniffed his armpit. He hoped he didn't smell too bad. Hiding out in that abandoned factory since yesterday did little for his hygiene. He wished he had been able to return home for a shower and clean clothes, but he didn't want to endanger his grandmother. He lifted his hand to knock on the door. He put his hand down and turned to go into the restroom. He stripped off his shirt and washed his face and under his arms with the soap in the dispenser. He dried himself with paper towels before putting his shirt back on. It wasn't much of an improvement, but he couldn't think of anything else to do. He returned to the door. This time he knocked. There was no answer. Smokey remembered, to see the Accountant, he needed to call before anyone would open the door. He pulled out his cell phone and punched in the number.

A large man holding a pistol opened the door. He recognized Smokey and motioned for him to enter. "What do you want?" The man asked, still holding the weapon in his hand as he closed the door.

Smokey cleared his throat. "Can I see the Accountant?"

"Wait here."

Smokey took two steps to stand aside the door. He wiped his hands on his pants again. The large individual returned. Smokey took a small step backwards.

The man signaled for Smokey to follow him. He led Smokey into the Accountant's office. The Accountant looked up from his computer and leaned back in his chair. "Why are you here? It's not time for you to make a deposit."

Smokey looked around, noting the two henchmen in the office. He wiped his hands on his trousers.

"You nervous about something?" the Accountant asked.

Smokey nodded his head slightly. "I've got a problem and I'm hoping you can help."

The Accountant waved his hand toward Smokey. "What's the problem?"

"Haj is looking for a green notebook. A friend of mine had it. I got a hold of it, and I was going to give it to Haj, but these two guys started chasing me. I lost the notebook, but I think I can get it back if these two goons would leave me alone."

The Accountant motioned for one of the henchmen to come over. They held a brief conference in whispers. The Accountant waved the henchman away. "These two guys, they wouldn't be JJ and Theo, would they?"

"Yeah," Smokey answered nodding.

"And you want me to tell these two to leave you alone."

"Yeah, sure," Smokey answered with excitement. "If I can get these guys off my back, I can get that notebook Haj wants, and everything will be cool."

The Accountant stared at Smokey for a moment. "Okay. What about what you told the cops?"

Smokey jerked his head around to see if the henchmen moved. "What cops? Yeah, I got picked up, but I didn't tell them anything. All they had on me was a trespassing charge. I went to court, but nothing happened. I got probation. I have to do community service. That's it."

The Accountant leaned forward, placing his elbows on his desk, and bringing his hand to his chin. "Where is this notebook?"

"I dumped it. I didn't want JJ or Theo to find it on me. But I know where it is."

"Where?"

"I threw it into some bushes. I went back later, but it wasn't there. . ."

"Don't tell me where it isn't," the Accountant demanded. "Tell me where it is."

"I think some of the people from the old folks' home found it."

"Old folks' home?'"

"Yeah," Smokey answered. "There is this old folks' home. Some of the people there went to Denise's funeral, she's my friend that was killed. Anyway, I think they found it. But I know them and I'm sure I can get it back from them."

The Accountant put his palms on his desk. "Look, I don't work for Haj, and he doesn't work for me. I provide a service, a service that is in jeopardy because of this notebook. You get me that notebook, and I'll get Haj to leave you alone, along with those two goons he's hired. But you need to get me that notebook before I do anything. Understand?"

Smokey nodded. "Yeah sure. But I need to get JJ and Theo off my back before I can do anything. Can you at least do that?"

"I'll see what I can do."

"Thanks."

The Accountant leaned back in his chair. He held up his hand. "One more thing. Why do you look like a street bum?"

"Been hiding out since yesterday," Smokey replied. He cleared his throat. "I know it's kind of out there, but I could use some bread, you know, to lay low for a day or two."

The Accountant opened a desk drawer and took out some money. He counted it out. "Here's two hundred dollars. It's a loan. You will pay it back, with interest. But for right now, find a hotel, take a shower, and get some food. It's best if you lay low until I can get Haj's goons off your tail."

Smokey took a small step forward and slowly reached for the money. "Thanks. I'll be sure to pay you back as soon as I can."

"I know you will," the Accountant replied with a smile.

CHAPTER THIRTY-EIGHT

"What a disappointment," Brenda said as she surveyed the Deerhill Shopping Mall. There were nine enclosures in the food court, but six of them were empty. Of the three open, one sold cookies, another was a sandwich shop, and third was a pizza stand. "This place is so dead. There are so few people here."

Dot parked her wheelchair next to Brenda. "I know what you mean. When I was in high school, this was a swinging place. There was a movie theater, but it's been closed for years. As well as the arcade. Also, did you notice all the empty stores. Even the big-name stores have left."

Joseph and Franklin came over to join Brenda and Dot. "What have you two been up to?" Joseph asked.

"Pondering world events, discussing our nation's economy, considering our chances of running for president," Brenda announced with false pride.

Dot snickered. "We were talking about how few people there are here."

"Well, there aren't many shops," Franklin said looking around. "I wonder what happened. Are they closing this place?"

"Who knows," Brenda answered. "But I wonder if there is enough business here to keep the place open. I've noticed people, but not many of them are carrying any kind of packages. It doesn't look like many of them are shopping."

"Of course, they're shopping," Franklin blurted out. "Why else would they be here?"

Dot maneuvered her wheelchair so she could focus on the shoppers at the stores. "A lot of single people. When I was young, I used to go shopping with friends or family. I never went by myself. It wasn't fun to shop alone. I mean if I needed something, I would go to the nearest Walmart and get it. This was the place to hang out and have fun. Yeah, we bought things, but we rarely knew what we wanted until we got here."

"You know what I noticed," Franklin said while waving his hand. "There aren't any kids working around here. When I was in high school, we all had part-time jobs working at fast-food restaurants, in stores, selling newspapers, doing lawn work, and things. But I haven't seen one kid here working. They all seem to be wandering around."

Brenda tilted her head. "I wonder why they are here. There isn't an arcade. The movie theater closed years ago. There's nothing here that would attract a person to come to here."

Dot turned to face Brenda. "Now that you mention it, I've seen more people here walking around for exercise than for shopping. It makes me wonder what keeps this place up and running."

"Well, they did have that big car sale out here a couple of weeks ago," Joseph replied. "Then there are those special holiday events like the Fourth of July festival."

Franklin stood up and tugged on his belt. "There's a festival here. Why didn't anybody tell me? Tell you all what, I'll go to the restroom and when I get back, we can go to the festival." Franklin turned and headed to the public restrooms.

Joseph chuckled. "He's going to be awfully disappointed when he gets back."

∞∞∞∞∞∞

Franklin leaned on his cane more than he wanted. His legs were sore from walking around the mall. He placed his cane next to the sinks before going to the urinals. He finished and turned. He reached out to the wall to steady himself. He took a breath and took a small step toward the sinks. Another man entered the restroom, walking pass Franklin to one of the stalls. Franklin shuffled to the sinks and washed his hands. He grabbed his cane and hurried. The man who had walked pass him seemed familiar. Franklin looked over his shoulder as he exited the restroom. The man had large earlobes, big because of the rings in the. Franklin didn't know why, but he knew the man was dangerous.

CHAPTER THIRTY-NINE

Teresa Simpson groaned as she made her way to the front door. She peered through front window to see a middle-aged, black man with a Hispanic woman. These people weren't from her neighborhood, but she knew who they were. She opened the front door but kept the screen door closed. "What do you want?" she demanded.

Stanford reached into his pocket. "Don't bother," Simpson barked. "I know who you are."

Stanford ignored her comments. "I'm Detective Stanford Agusta and this is my partner Detective Catherine Diaz. I'm guessing you're Ms. Teresa Simpson, grandmother to Samuel Corden, also known as Smokey."

"Lucky you," Simpson hissed. "I know you're cops. So, what do you want? Samuel isn't here. And I don't know where he is."

Stanford heaved a heavy breath. Cat stepped forward, motioning for Stanford to give her some room. "Ms. Simpson, I realize you may not like police officers, but we're here to help your grandson."

"Bull," Simpson blurted out. "The cops don't want to help anyone down here. The only time a cop comes to this neighborhood is to arrest somebody. You just being here puts my grandson in danger. The sooner you leave the better."

"No," Stanford replied with a commanding voice. "I understand you don't like us, but we really are trying to help Smokey. He's in danger, and it's not from the police. Right now, we're the only ones who can keep him safe."

"He's telling you the truth," Cat said as she placed her hand on Stanford's sleeve. "We believe Smokey is in great danger and we want to help him."

Simpson glared at the detectives. "I know how you want to help him. You'll take him away and make him testify against someone. Someone who will be out on the streets and gunning for him before the day is done. He has a better chance on his own. If you really want to help him, leave. Leave right now."

Cat glanced at Stanford before facing Ms. Simpson. "Very well Ms. Simpson. We'll leave, but I'm sure we'll be back. Unfortunately, it will probably be to inform you of the death of your grandson. Before we leave, won't you please reconsider."

Simpson opened the screen door and spat at Cat's feet. "Get out of here. The police are as useful as that old shoe factory on Redwood Avenue." She closed the screen door and slammed the front door shut.

Stanford and Cat returned to their vehicle. Cat slid into the passenger seat and waited for Stanford to get comfortable behind the wheel of the car. "Where to now?" she asked.

Stanford put the key in the ignition and buckled his seatbelt. "We cruise around and hope we spot Smokey, unless you have a better idea,"

Cat shook her head. "Not at the moment."

CHAPTER FORTY

Haj watched the old people puttering around the mall. He could hear them complaining about how few people were there. Haj looked at his cell phone. They were late. Haj didn't like waiting. His phone rang.

"You're late," Haj said. "You wanted to meet here and you're late. Where are you?"

"We're here, but we're hanging out a few stores down from where you are," the other party answered. "Give us a few minutes. There's a problem. Wait. They left. We'll be there in a minute."

Haj ended the call and looked around. He saw JJ and Theo approaching, watching the old folks walk away. They waited until the group was out of sight before coming over to Haj.

"What's going on?" Haj demanded. "You're late."

"Sorry about that," JJ said as he and Theo watched the direction the old people had gone. "Did you see those old people that were here a few minutes ago?"

Haj snickered. "Of course. How can I miss them? There's like six people here. It's kind of hard to miss anyone. This is why I hate coming to this place. Too many security cameras and not very many people. Tend to really stand out here. Meeting here is a bad idea."

"Yeah, well, today it worked to our advantage," Theo responded. "We were coming over when we saw those old people."

Haj grinned. "And they're from that old age home where you broke in. You were afraid they would recognize you. I thought you said you took care of the person who saw you."

"We did," JJ replied. "But the person who we snatched was in that group. We couldn't take the chance of him recognizing us."

Haj raised his head and stared at JJ before looking in the direction the group had gone. "You mean the guy who saw me kill Denise was in that group of old folks?'

"Yeah," JJ answered.

"He was the old man walking with the cane, " Theo added. "He had kind of a limp. Did you see him?"

Haj snorted. "Yeah, I saw him. I was in the restroom and I noticed he was staring at me. Figured he some kind of pervert. Now I know. He recognized me." Haj stood up and picked up his cell phone. "Come on. We've got to leave. Where are you guys parked."

Theo pointed to the way they had come from. "Down there."

Haj was already moving in that direction. "Let's go. The sooner we get out of here, the better."

∞∞∞∞∞∞

Dot and the others entered the clothing store. "My goodness. Look at those jeans," Dot said. "There are more holes in them than there are actual jeans."

"I couldn't wear anything like that," Brenda added. "I would never be able to get my feet through the right hole. I'd end up tripping over myself."

Joseph pointed to a jacket with lots of sequins on it. "What about that coat. You'd shine like a disco ball." Joseph pantomimed disco movements, bringing giggles from the two ladies.

Joseph turned to Franklin. "What's wrong old buddy?" Joseph asked with a chuckle. "We're not too old to boogie."

Franklin stared at shoes on a shelf next to the clothes. "Those shoes."

Brenda looked at the shoes. "Blue shoes. Where would you wear blue shoes?"

"Don't step on my blue-suede shoes," Joseph sang as he continued to dance around.

"No, not me," Franklin declared. "Those are the shoes that poor girl was wearing when she was killed."

Dot maneuvered her chair to face Franklin. "It's okay dear. We all feel bad about that poor girl and what happened to her."

Franklin's eye opened wide. He turned to face the others. He shook his hand at them. "No, it's not that," he uttered. "I think I saw the killer. He's right here. I saw him in the restroom."

CHAPTER FORTY-ONE

William pulled into the Comfort Cottages parking lot. Jennifer got out of the passenger side while William went to help Melissa out of his car.

"Thank you, young man," Melissa said as she extended her hand to William. "It's nice to have a gentleman around."

Jennifer came up to William and put her arm around his. "Melissa's right. It's nice to have you around."

Melissa straightened up. "For some reason, I think Jennifer's reason for appreciating your presence is not the same as mine." Melissa gently patted William's chest. "Still, I'm delighted that you're here."

"My pleasure," William replied.

Jennifer twisted slightly toward William and smiled. "I'm happy you're here too." Jennifer turned to face Melissa. She cleared her throat.

"No need for that, dear," Melissa said. "I'm old, but I haven't forgotten that a man and a woman prefer to be alone. As they say, two is company, but three is a crowd. So, *this crowd is going in and leaving this company alone.*"

Jennifer leaned into William and placed her head on his shoulder as she watched Melissa walk into the building. Jennifer lifted her head and looked at William. "Thank you for coming with us this morning."

"My pleasure."

Jennifer turned, facing William. She smiled. She continued to hold onto William's arm. He brought his other hand around to take Jennifer's hands. He stood as silent as a statue. Jennifer could feel his heavy breathing.

"There you are," a familiar voice bellowed, breaking Jennifer's moment with William. Susan ran up to Jennifer. "Franklin found him. He found him."

"Found who?" William asked.

"The killer," Susan shouted. "Franklin found him."

Jennifer let go of William. "Where is he?"

Susan relaxed her shoulders. "Who? Franklin or the killer?"

"Let's start with Franklin," Jennifer said with exasperation.

Susan lifted her head. "He's in the rec room. He's telling everyone how he found the killer."

Jennifer rushed pass Susan. William and Susan followed her into the building. The three of them hurried through the lobby into the rec room where they found Franklin surrounded by several of the residents. "Franklin. What happened?" Jennifer shouted.

Franklin glared at the interruption. "I was just telling everyone what happened."

"Calm down, Franklin," Brenda said as she approached Jennifer. Brenda placed a hand on Jennifer's arm. "We were at the mall when Franklin saw the man who killed that poor girl."

"Did you call the police?" Jennifer yelled. "Have they caught him?"

"Well, we were going to, but we lost him," Brenda answered.

Jennifer closed her eyes and shook her head. She opened her eyes, took a deep breath. "You're not making sense. You found the killer, then you lost him. What happened?"

"That's what I was telling everyone until you interrupted me," Franklin said, holding his head high. Jennifer motioned for him to continue. "Brenda, Dot, Joseph, and I went to the mall this afternoon."

Jennifer stiffened her shoulders. "What were you doing at the mall?"

"What's wrong with us going to the mall?" Franklin demanded. "We have a right to go if we want. We're not prisoners here."

"You're quite right," Jennifer said, holding her hands in front of her. "Please continue with what happened while you were at the mall."

Pleased with himself, Franklin held his head up higher. "While we were at the mall, I used the restroom. It wasn't very crowded. Did you know that hardly anyone goes to the mall anymore? Anyway, I saw the killer in the restroom."

"Franklin didn't recognize him at first," Brenda added. "We were walking around the mall when we saw a display in one of the stores. There were blue shoes, which reminded Franklin of the woman that was murdered. That's when he realized he had seen the killer in the restroom."

"I'm telling the story," Franklin shouted. Franklin took a deep breath before speaking. "Once I remembered I saw the killer, we all went back to where I saw him. But he was gone. We searched the mall, but we didn't see him again. After that, we came back here."

"Did you call the police?" William asked.

"Why?" Brenda questioned. "The killer was gone. What could they do?"

"They could have checked the security cameras," William replied.

"That wouldn't help," Brenda argued. "Franklin is the only one who can recognize the killer."

William nodded. "Yes, but they can have Franklin review the tapes with them."

"That's right," Franklin declared. "I can recognize him. Then the police can arrest him."

Melissa cleared her throat. "While that would help the police, but only if they know who he is. Having a picture of a suspect is not the same as knowing who he is. It is a step in the right direction, but we still don't know who the killer is, and why that poor girl was murdered."

Jennifer placed herself between Franklin, Brenda, and William. "Let's not argue. The first thing we should do is call the police so that they can get the security tapes."

"Then I'll find the killer," Franklin proudly stated.

CHAPTER FORTY-TWO
(day fourteen)

Stanford took a bite of his apple fritter before placing it back on the napkin on his desk. "How much longer before our witness shows up?"

"Give the guy a break," Cat pleaded. "He's an old man. When I called the home, the manager, Jennifer Stebbins said they would be here right after breakfast. By the way, don't eat all the donuts. They may want one when they get here."

Stanford grunted. "Do you have the tapes set up?"

"Everything's set."

"What's set?" Franklin asked as he entered Stanford's and Cat's office. Franklin immediately went over to the pictures on Cat's bulletin board. "Who's the artist?"

"My daughter," Cat answered, "she five."

"I like it," Franklin said. "So, why did you want me to come down here?"

Jennifer stepped beside Franklin. "We're here to look at security tapes from the mall where you were yesterday?"

Franklin gave her a confused look. "Why are we looking at security tapes?'

Stanford snickered. "We were hoping you would be able to point out the killer. You said you saw him yesterday at the mall."

"Yes, I did," Franklin shouted. "I saw him when I was using the restroom. I was with some friends from Comfort Cottages. We went back to find him, but he was gone."

"Yes, we know," Stanford replied. "Now, if you come over here, Detective Diaz will show you the security tapes we got from the mall. Let us know if you recognize anyone."

Franklin nodded he understood as he sat down in front of the computer. Cat started the program to show the security tapes.

Jennifer stood behind Franklin watching the tapes. "Why are these pictures so blurry? I've seen photographs from satellites that show such clear shots of the earth, and those are from thousands of miles away. Yet, these are so blurry. It's hard to see anyone's face."

Most businesses buy the least expensive cameras they can," Cat answered. "The result is those cameras don't have the resolution of the ones in space. Also, many times people wear sunglasses, facemasks, and hats; all of which make it harder to identify a person. Still, sometimes, we get lucky."

Franklin leaned forward and studied the tapes. For more than an hour, he sat focused on the images on the computer screen.

"That's the last of the tapes," Cat said as she ended the computer program. "Did you see anyone you recognized?"

Franklin pointed to the computer. "Can I see the part where we were sitting at the table?' Cat accessed the program and ran it forward to the section Franklin requested. Franklin touched the screen. "Maybe that's him."

"Maybe?" Stanford interjected.

"I really can't tell," Franklin said. "I can't see his ears on this thing. But I think he's the same person who came out of the restroom after I did."

Cat ran the program forward a bit more. "Do you recognize the two men who joined the guy you pointed out?"

Franklin shook his head.

Jennifer leaned over Franklin's shoulder to get a better look at the images on the screen. "I wish these pictures were a bit clearer. I don't recognize anyone, but I can't really see their faces."

"That's okay," Stanford said. "Believe it or not, you've been a big help."

Franklin snorted. "Don't patronize me. Sorry I could point out the killer. But if you had better pictures, I could have."

Cat placed her arm on Franklin's shoulder. "No, really. You did help us."

Franklin stood up and glared at Cat. "Just because I'm an old man you feel you have to treat me like someone who needs to be coddled. Well, you don't."

Jennifer stepped over to Franklin. "You're right. Look, you did your best. I couldn't pick anyone out of the tapes either. It's not your fault."

"Damn right," Franklin declared.

Jennifer gently took Franklin's arm. "I think that's all we can do for the police at the moment. Why don't we go back home?"

Franklin nodded in agreement and started for the door. Jennifer thanked the detectives before she followed Franklin out.

After they exited, Stanford faced Cat. "I hope we didn't upset him too much. He really did give us a lead. Did you recognize the two others that joined the person he pointed out?"

"Well, like the lady said, it's hard to see their faces. But they did remind me of the two we had in here a few days ago. I think it's time we talk to JJ and Theo again."

"I agree," Stanford answered.

CHAPTER FORTY-THREE

The waitress looked up as JJ and Theo entered the diner. She looked over to Haj, who was seated in the back booth. He motioned for her it was okay. She knew if he wanted anything from her, he would let her know. JJ and Theo slid into the booth, opposite Haj.

"We're here," JJ said. "What's up?"

"Thanks for the heads up yesterday," Haj answered. "Now, we need to discuss what to do."

Theo fiddled with the condiments on the table. "What do you mean? Has the job changed?"

Haj stared at the two. "No, the job hasn't changed. I still want you to take care of that old man and get me that notebook."

"Taking care of the old man is one thing," JJ said. "But getting that notebook is another. We don't know where it is.'

"When did you see it last?" Haj asked.

Theo shrugged his shoulders. "We might have seen it with Smokey."

"So, get Smokey," Haj hissed.

"He's hiding, and no one knows where," JJ replied.

Haj placed his elbows on the table and leaned forward. "Listen, you find Smokey and get that notebook. And get rid of that old man. I don't care how you do it."

"Yeah, we understand," JJ said in a low voice. "The problem is finding Smokey, then finding that old man where he's alone. We weren't going to kill him at the mall in front of witnesses and security cameras."

Haj scratched his ear. "There is one way you can find Smokey. He's really close to his grandmother. She's raised him ever since his mother died and his father left. If anyone knows how to find Smokey, she will. Talk to the grandmother."

Theo clasped his hands in front of himself. "What if she doesn't want to talk to us?"

Haj pointed a finger at Theo. "Then you make her talk to you. Find Smokey and that notebook."

JJ put his hand on Theo's arm and motioned for him to lean back. "You're making this job harder," JJ said to Haj. "Instead of one person, we may have to take care of Smokey and the grandmother too."

"Tell you what," Haj responded. "Get that notebook and that old man. If anyone gets in your way, deal with it. And to show you how understanding I can be, I'll double what I offered you."

"Triple it," JJ said. "After all, there's a good chance we'll have to deal with three people instead of just one."

Haj stared at JJ for a moment before answering. "Okay. Triple. But I want results or you get nothing. And remember this, I may not be so agreeable to your terms in the future. Now, get out of here and do your job."

JJ smiled as he and Theo slid out of the booth and left the diner.

∞∞∞∞∞∞

"You sure this is Smokey's place?" JJ asked.

"Yeah, I'm sure," Theo answered.

"We'll play it cool, say we're Smokey's friends and sent to help him. We can even say we're here to pick up the notebook for him" JJ flicked his head in the direction of the house to signal for them to get out of the car. "Let's go. Let me do the talking."

They walked up to the door. JJ was about to press the doorbell when the front door opened. Behind the screen door stood an elderly woman in a flower print dress.

"What do you want?" She demanded leaning on her walker.

JJ waved his hand and smiled. "You're Mrs. Simpson, Smokey's grandmother?"

"Yes, I'm Teresa Simpson. Samuel's my grandson. So, why do you ask?"

We're friends of Smokey. He sent us over to pick up something for him, a green notebook."

"I don't know nothing about a green notebook," the woman said while staring at JJ and Theo.

"Maybe he left it in his room," JJ suggested.

"No, he didn't," Simpson replied with hostility in her voice. "Who are you?"

JJ waved his hand to include him and Theo. "Like I told you. We're Smokey's friends. Maybe if you could tell us where he is, we could go there and he can get the notebook for us."

"You're no friends of his. I'm his grandma and I know all his friends. I've never seen you before. Besides, he wouldn't send two white boys to this neighborhood to do anything for him. So, you two better leave before things become unpleasant for you both."

"Listen lady," Theo snapped. "Just tell us where Smokey is. We'll take it from there."

"Kiss off," she replied. "I don't know where he is and even if I did, I wouldn't tell you."

Theo grabbed the screen door handle and yanked it open. He pushed his way in. JJ followed. Theo pushed the old woman back into the house. "Lady, we wanted to be nice, but you're not helping."

"What are you going to do?" Simpson demanded, trying to hide the fear in her voice.

"You're going to call Smokey and arrange for us to meet him," JJ answered.

"What if I don't?"

JJ leaned closer to the woman. "You're going to arrange for us to meet Smokey. The question is whether or not it's at your funeral or someplace else."

CHAPTER FORTY-FOUR

The hotel room was clean but not very comfortable. The air conditioner hissed out a stream of air but failed to cool the room. The windows opened, but the noise and air from the street only made things worse. The walls were thin, so Smokey could hear everything happening in the rooms next door. The TV worked but the sound was terrible. Smokey's cell phone rang. He jumped to answer it.

"Hello. Is this the Accountant?"

"Accountant? Who's the Accountant?"

"Grandma," Smokey shouted. "What's wrong? Why are you calling me?"

"We need to meet," a strange voice answered.

"Who is this?" Smokey yelled.

"Calm down. It's me, JJ. Listen, Theo and I are at your grandmother's home."

"You do anything to hurt her, I'll kill you," Smokey shouted.

"I said calm down. No one wants to hurt the old lady. You do what we ask, no problem. We let her go. No hard feelings."

"What do you want?"

"We need that green notebook that you have. Just bring it over here, and we leave."

Smokey pulled his phone down to his thigh while he took a breath. He brought it back up to his mouth. "I don't have it."

"That's too bad. Without that notebook, things don't look good for your grandma."

"Wait," Smokey shouted. "I know where it is. It'll take me a while to get it. Just don't hurt my grandma."

"Call us when you get it. We'll be with your grandmother." JJ ended the call.

"What now?" Simpson asked. "Are you going to move in here until Samuel comes home?"

"Stay there," Theo said as he left the room. A few minutes later he returned with Ms. Simpson's coat and a full plastic bag.

"What's in the bag?" JJ asked.

"Her medication. Don't want her to die on us before we get that notebook."

"Good thinking," JJ said.

"What are you going to do?" Ms. Simpson asked as she took a few steps back.

"You're coming with us," JJ replied.

"Why not just stay here? Why take me someplace? What's wrong with waiting here in my home?"

JJ grinned. "So that you can poison us, or sneak a message out to a neighbor, or pull a knife on us. No way. We're taking you someplace where we control the situation, not you."

Simpson raised her head. "And how is Samual going to find us? He'll come home and find no one. What do you think he'll do then with this notebook that you're after?"

JJ stepped closer to the old woman. "I'm hoping he'll call you. Then we can tell him where to meet us."

CHAPTER FORTY-FIVE

Dot sat to the right of the entrance for Comfort Cottages. She enjoyed sitting outside in the fresh air and shade. The wind gently moved the leaves in the trees and the petals of the flowers. This peaceful moment was shattered with the arrival of a blue hatchback screeching to a halt in a parking space. Smokey jumped out of the car. He came to an abrupt stop at the entrance of the building.

Dot maneuvered her chair to approach Smokey. "Well, this is a surprise. What brings you back here?"

Smokey let out a small cough. "I need to talk to somebody here. Who's in charge?"

"Jennifer Stebbins." Dot said as she motioned for Smokey to follow her inside. "You know that."

"Well, I've got to see her. It's a matter of life and death."

Dot wheeled her chair around to face Smokey. "Hold on young man. Whatever it is, it can wait the five minutes it takes to get inside."

Smokey waved his hands and fell in behind Dot as she progressed toward Jennifer's office. They entered her office and found it empty. "Where is she?" Smokey yelled. "We need to find her."

"Calm down. We will. She's here in the building. Good grief, hold your horses."

"What's going on?" a voice behind them demanded. Smokey and Dot turned to find Susan standing with her hands on her hips.

"We need to find Jennifer," Dot answered. "Do you know where she is?"

"She's in the rec room. Wait one minute and I'll get her."

Susan walked away. Smokey took a couple of steps to follow her until Dot grabbed his arm. "Stay here," she said. "It'll only be a moment. Perhaps you could tell me what the problem is."

"Who said there was a problem?" Smokey stated.

"You did when you came running in here demanding to speak to Jennifer. You're too emotional for this to be anything but a problem, and I'll bet it's a serious one."

Smokey wiped his face with his hand as he shuffled back and forth in front of the office. Jennifer approached Dot and Smokey. Smokey stood still, staring at her, William and Susan showed up but remained standing several feet behind Jennifer.

Jennifer crossed her arms "I understand you wanted to talk to me. What about?"

Smokey looked around, noting each of the individuals present. "Can I talk to you alone? It's kind of private."

Jennifer led Smokey into her office and closed the door. She walked around her desk to her chair. She signaled to Smokey to take a seat.

Smokey sat down and wiped his hands on his pants. "A friend of mine, Denise, was killed a couple of weeks ago. A couple of days ago, they held a funeral for her."

"I know," Jennifer replied. "I sorry for your loss. Several of our residents also attended her funeral."

"Yeah, that's right," Smokey said, moving forward in his chair. "At the funeral, I got a green notebook from one of the people who worked with Denise. Somehow, I lost it. I really need to find it. It's very important. I think maybe one of your people who were at the funeral found it. If you could have them give it back to me, that would be great. It's really very important I get it back. You see, it belongs to someone else, and I promised him I would get it for him."

"May I ask why this notebook is so important?"

"I really can't say. I know it's important, but I really don't know why."

Jennifer picked up a pen and twirled in her hands as she leaned back in her chair. She watched Smokey for a few seconds before responding. "It turns out one of our residents did find a green notebook. It could be the one you're looking for. Is there any way you could identify it? I mean, green notebooks are common. How will we know if this is the one you need?"

"Oh, I can tell. I've seen the notebook and if it's the one I'm looking for, I'll know it."

Jennifer got up from her desk and opened the door to her office. She wasn't surprised to find Dot, William, and Susan waiting in the hall. Jennifer addressed Susan and asked her to find Franklin.

"What's up?" William asked.

Jennifer glanced back at Smokey before responding to William. "Nothing to worry about. The young man in my office is trying to locate some lost property."

Dot gasped. She turned her wheelchair and started down the hall towards her room. Jennifer and William watched as she left. A few minutes later, Susan returned with Franklin.

"What's up?" Franklin asked as soon as he saw William.

"I asked for you," Jennifer interrupted. "If you come into my office, I have someone who would like to talk to you."

Franklin followed Jennifer. He saw Smokey sitting in front of Jennifer's desk. "I know you," Franklin said.

Smokey stood up. "No kidding. I've been here enough times."

"Listen up," Jennifer commanded. She faced Franklin. "This young man lost a green notebook a few days ago when he attended the funeral that you, along with others, attended. Remember, it was for that poor girl that was murdered a couple of weeks ago. The one you saw that night. It happened in the parking lot of the restaurant behind us."

Franklin looked down at the floor. He put his hand to his chin and took a couple of breaths. He put down his hand, stared at Smokey. "Yes, I remember. The killer beat her up. But it wasn't this guy. The killer was a white guy."

"Yes, I know," Jennifer acknowledged. "But a few days ago, you found a green notebook. Do you remember what you did with the notebook?"

"Notebook?" a confused Franklin responded.

Dot came rolling into the office. "Yes, Franklin. This notebook. Remember? You found it and you gave it to me."

Frankin took the notebook from Dot and opened it. His face lit up with recognition. "Yes, I found this. It was in some bushes. But we didn't know what the numbers were for."

"That's right," Dot said as she retrieved the notebook from Franklin's hand. She turned to face Jennifer. "You know I love puzzles, and I used to be an accountant. We thought it might be some kind of ledger, but we couldn't figure it out."

"Who cares," Smokey asserted. "It's my notebook and I want it back."

"Not a chance," Dot declared. "It is a ledger and I'm certain it contains information about some kind of illegal activity, probably drugs."

"You're crazy," Smokey bellowed.

Dot held the notebook against her chest. "Fine. Then tell me exactly what the numbers mean, *if it is your book.*"

"All right, it's not mine. It belongs to a friend and he needs it back. I don't know what the numbers mean, but it doesn't have anything to do with drugs." Smokey grabbed the notebook, turned, and stopped

William was leaning against the doorframe with Susan standing next to him. He pointed to the notebook. William took the notebook from Smokey's hands and handed it back to Dot. Smokey returned to the chair in front of Jennifer's desk. "Were you able to figure out what the numbers meant?" William asked.

"Naturally," Dot claimed with pride. "Thank goodness for Google." She opened the notebook to a page and pointed to an entry. These entries here followed the pattern for a date; the day, the month, and the year. I noticed the entries had the last four digits of *5782*. So, I googled that number. It's the year of *5782* for the Hebrew calendar. Then I remembered that the funeral was a Jewish ceremony, which meant the girl that was murdered was Jewish. I did a bit of research and found out the Jewish New Year is in September. Starting with September, which is the month of *Elul*, I counted it as the first month. Using the pattern of day, month, year; I was able to figure out the dates of the entries. For example, here we have 06/11/5782, the sixth day of the month Tammuz in the year of 5782 according to the Hebrew calendar. But that date in the calendar we use is the tenth of July of this year, 2022. That was the first part of the puzzle."

"Are you sure of that?" William asked.

"Well, I didn't do it with every date in the notebook, but I did it with enough to be sure. Besides, as you go through the entries, you can see there are several for the same date and the same month."

"What else did you find?" Jennifer asked

Dot pointed to a column of figures. "This column is obviously money. The difficult part was this column. It contained two letters and a number. I remembered the woman that was killed. Her name was Denise Linden. And this young man's real name is Samuel Corden. There are some entries here: DL1 and DL2, as well as SC1 and SC2. I'm guessing these mean Denise Linden and Samuel Corden. There are other entries, probably for the names of other people. The numbers are locations known to the person who owns the notebook and the people listed in it. Of course, I could be wrong, but I doubt it. Then we can always ask Samuel here."

William stared at Smokey. No one spoke. After a few minutes of silence, Smokey glared at William. "I have no idea about anything in that notebook. It's not even mine."

"Then why do you want it?" Jennifer asked.

"I need it. I have to get it back to the owner."

William leaned over and took the notebook from Dot. "I think it's better if we give it to the police. They can figure out if it's really evidence or not." William turned to Smokey. "If it is, you might be in trouble. That's why you want it."

"No," Smokey shouted.

William held the notebook up. "Then why do you want it?"

"Like I said, I need to give it back to the owner."

Jennifer leaned against her desk and crossed her arms. "Why do you need to return it to the owner? Can't the owner come here and claim it?"

Smokey stood up. "Hey, if you're not going to give me the notebook, then screw you. I'm out of here." He started toward the door.

William put up his hand and forced Smokey back into the office. "You're not going anywhere."

"You can't keep me here," Smokey shouted. "That's kidnapping."

William shrugged his shoulders. "Okay. Then let's call the police. They can come and arrest us while they rescue you."

Smokey looked around at everyone. "Just let me go. You can keep the notebook."

William continued to block the door. "For some reason, I think you're hiding something. You really need this notebook, and it's not because you're a boy scout and doing a good deed by returning it to its owner. What's the real story?"

Jennifer walked over and took the notebook from William. "Everyone, out of my office. This young man and I will settle this matter."

"But Jennifer," Susan objected. "He's a drug dealer."

"No, he's a young man with a problem," Jennifer stated. "And the best way to resolve this issue is for everyone to leave. Now go!"

William stepped away from the door, allowing Dot and Franklin to exit Jennifer's office. Jennifer closed the door. William, Susan, Franklin, and Dot stayed in the hall for a few moments until Dot suggested they wait in the rec room.

Jennifer returned to her chair behind the desk. Smokey also sat down. Jennifer placed the notebook on the top of her desk, but she kept one hand on it. "What is really happening?"

"I don't know what you mean."

"I mean what is the real reason you are here? I understand you want this notebook. It's obviously something that can get someone, including you, in a lot of trouble. But there's more to it. Let me ask you this. Are you in trouble? Do you need some help?"

"I don't need any help. I just need that notebook."

Jennifer opened a drawer in her desk and threw the notebook in it. "I'll give you the notebook when you tell me the truth and tell me why it's so important."

Smokey turned and stormed out of the office. William, Dot, and Susan heard him cursing as he left the building.

CHAPTER FORTY-SIX

"I have to go to the bathroom," Ms. Simpson yelled.

"Be quiet old woman," JJ shouted back.

"No, I won't. You two kidnap me, drag me to this old factory, and tie me up. I'm stuck in this chair, which is uncomfortable, and you expect me to just sit here. What about some food, some water, and I still need to go to the bathroom."

JJ stood up in front the folding chair he was sitting in, turned, and glared at the old woman. He and Theo had tied her to a chair with four stationary legs. She sat against a painted green concrete wall, the only one without any doorways. JJ and Theo had set up a folding table and chairs, waiting for Smokey to call. They had been there for several hours and all three of them were becoming impatient.

The cell phone on the table rang. JJ grabbed it. "It's about time," he hissed into the phone. "You got the book?"

"No," Smokey answered.

"What!" Smokey could hear the anger in JJ's voice. "Then why are you calling?"

"I almost had it," Smokey said with a slight quiver in his voice. "I went to that old-folks home. One of them picked it up at Denise's funeral. The woman in charge of the place took it and wouldn't give it to me. She's still got it."

"Why didn't you just take it from her?" a frustrated JJ said.

"I tried, but this big dude stopped me. He blocked me in. Then he took it away from me and gave it to that woman."

"Is that my grandson," Ms. Simpson yelled. "Don't give them anything."

Theo rushed over and stuffed a rag in the woman's mouth. "Be quiet you old bitch. You don't want us to hurt you."

Ms. Simpson spit the rag out. "No, I won't. You don't scare me. . ."

Theo took the rag and placed it over her mouth, trying it behind her head.

"Hey, don't you hurt my grandma," Smokey shouted.

JJ took a breath before continuing his conversation. "Listen. Your grandmother will be okay once we get that notebook. Quit fooling around and get it. You have until midnight to get it to us."

"Midnight! That's less than ten hours from now. It's impossible."

"Make it possible. If not, your grandmother won't see tomorrow's sunrise. Have I made myself clear?"

"Yeah, you're clear," Smokey said. "But if anything happens to my grandma, I'll kill you."

JJ laughed. "If you don't get that notebook, you're welcome to try. It will make things a lot easier for us." JJ ended the call.

Theo removed the rag from the woman's mouth.

She looked up at him, then spit at his feet. "Think you're a tough guy? Well, you're not."

"Shut her up," JJ demanded.

"Why don't you shut me up," she yelled. "And I still need to go to the bathroom."

Theo reached behind her and untied her. "Let's go. And afterwards, I'm bringing you back here and you shut up. It's bad enough we have wait around without you making all sorts of noise."

JJ waited until Theo took the old woman out of the room. He picked up the cell phone and punched in a phone number. The phone at the other end rang twice before someone answered. "Yeah," the voice at the other end said.

JJ looked around to make sure he was alone. "Haj, we have a problem."

CHAPTER FORTY-SEVEN

The evening meal at Comfort Cottages was the highlight of the day and a disappointment. Unless residents made arrangements to dine out, they all gathered in the dining room. This was when most residents socialized with each other. Their daily lives were fairly uneventful, so the main topic at the meal was the food. They always compared each entre to some homemade dish they used to make when they were raising their families. The main course was too bland, too dry, or too runny. The side dishes always needed more seasoning. And dessert was unusually too sweet and too small. On the rare occasion when an individual had something to say other than complaining about the food, he or she became the center of attention. The residents welcomed any change or deviation of their daily routine.

Smokey was counting on the residents being focused on their evening meal. He parked his car down the street, out of view of the facility. He made sure he approached the building from the edge of the parking lot, staying out of sight of the front entrance. A check of the entry way revealed no one. He was able to enter the building without anyone seeing him.

Too many times, the best plans fail because of someone being where he or she shouldn't be or wasn't expected. David Richards and Kevin Batters arrived at Comfort Cottages three minutes after Smokey went into the building. The two firefighter buddies of William were carrying a cold, six-pack of Corona beer, a large bag of potato chips, and a bag of cheeseburgers from a local drive through. They entered the building and were on their way to the dining hall when they heard noises coming from an office. The sign identified the office as Jennifer Stebbins'. However, the current occupant was a teenage black man. David and

Kevin carefully set their packages down on two chairs in the lobby before they approached the doorway of the office.

"Hey buddy, what are you looking for?" Kevin asked.

Smokey froze, took a breath, and straightened up. "I was sent in here to get something. Who are you?"

"A couple of friends of the manager," David answered. "So, who are you?"

"I work here," Smokey answered. "Just started this week."

Two tours in Afghanistan taught Kevin when people don't answer a specific question, something is not right. He stepped forward and put out his hand. "I'm Kevin. David and I work with William."

Smokey shook Kevin's hand. "Nice to meet you."

"Nice to meet you too," Kevin responded. "So, what is your name? What should we call you?"

Smokey hesitated before replying. "JJ. My friends call me JJ."

Kevin still held on to Smokey's hand. He could feel Smokey's sweaty palm. The moment's hesitation was all Kevin needed to know Smokey was lying. "What are you looking for?" Kevin asked. "Maybe we can help you find it."

Smokey released Kevin's hand. He wiped his hand on the front of his trousers. "Nah, that's okay. I've got it taken care of."

David crossed his arms over his chest as he leaned against the door frame. He remained silent, staring at Smokey. Kevin took a couple of steps back before placing his hands on his hips. Both men remained in the office.

"I've got it covered," Smokey stated in an assertive voice.

Neither of the firefighters moved.

"What's your problem?" Smokey demanded. "You need to get out of here."

"Tell you what," David said as he pointed to Smokey. "We'll follow you out."

"You two don't belong here," Smokey argued. "Now leave."

David gave a single word response. "Nope."

Smokey stood up as tall as he could while placing his hands on his hips. "What is your problem? I work here. You don't. Now get out of this office."

Kevin looked at David. "You got this covered?" David nodded that he did. "Then, I'll go and get someone who works here to handle this."

"I work here," Smokey shouted.

"That's right, he does," a voice behind the two men replied. They turned to see Jennifer standing behind them. She stepped around David, moving next to Kevin. "This is Samual Corden, also known as Smokey. He's supposed to do a hundred hours of community service here."

Kevin motioned with his hand toward Smokey. "He told us his name was JJ. We were curious about what he was doing in your office."

Jennifer walked over to Smokey and pulled him away from behind her desk. "He was looking for a notebook, one that came into my possession this afternoon."

"It's not yours," Smokey asserted. "I need to get it back to the person who lost it."

Jennifer put up her hand to signal Kevin and David to remain quiet. "Gentlemen, I'll take care of this. Why don't you go to see William? I'm sure he'll be happy to see you." The two men nodded and left Jennifer with Smokey. She motioned for Smokey to close the office door.

Jennifer waited until Smokey complied before she sat down. Smokey took a seat in front of Jennifer's desk. "Are you ready to tell me why you need this notebook?" Jennifer queried.

Smokey took a deep breath and exhaled through his nose. "All I can tell you is I need that notebook. I have to get it back to somebody. It's a matter of life and death."

"If that is the case, maybe we should call the police."

"No," Smokey yelled. "If the cops show up, my grandma is dead."

Jennifer stared at Smokey for a few minutes. "I think I understand. Someone, the person who wants the notebook, has your grandmother. If you bring the notebook to him, he will let your grandmother go. Is that right?"

Smokey gave Jennifer a slight nod. "Something like that."

Jennifer pulled the notebook out of the drawer. "I'll give you the notebook. But I'm quite sure whoever has your grandmother will not let her go. In all probability, he will kill both you and her."

"That's my problem," Smokey said with resentment.

"Wait here," Jennifer commanded as she stood up. "I'll be right back." She took the notebook and walked out of her office. Smokey started to get up. He changed his mind and sat back down.

After several minutes, Jennifer returned. In her hands were the notebook and several sheets of paper. Jennifer walked around her desk and sat down. She folded two of the sheets of paper and placed them in the notebook before handing it to Smokey. "Here is the notebook. But notice that there are two sheets of paper in there. They are copies of the pages of the notebook. Let whoever wants that notebook know there are copies of it. Call it insurance that he doesn't kill you or your grandmother. It's important for him to know that if anything happens to you, or your grandmother, the copies go straight to the police."

Smokey looked at the notebook and the two pages. "How do I know I can trust you?"

"You don't. But think about it. Why would I want to hurt you or your grandmother? I have nothing to gain."

Smokey remained silent.

"I realize this puts you in a tough spot, since the person who wants that notebook wants all the evidence in his control. But that gives him control of the situation, which means he can do anything he wants, and that includes killing you."

Smokey stood up and went to the door. He turned to Jennifer. "Thanks. But I have to tell you, this isn't a good idea. He'll probably come after you for those copies."

"Who's he?"

"Someone you don't want to meet," Smokey said as he left Jennifer.

CHAPTER FORTY-EIGHT

Jennifer walked into the dining room to find Franklin drinking a beer and sitting with William, David, and Kevin. Franklin was also enjoying a cheeseburger and managed to drop some ketchup on his shirt. She noticed Susan was sitting next to William. She was also drinking a beer. William waved for Jennifer to join the group. He offered Jennifer the last beer in the six-pack. Jennifer accepted it without hesitation.

"Looks like we'll have to make another beer run," Kevin said with a chuckle.

"Damn right," Franklin eagerly agreed. "One beer is just enough to wet the whistle. This time bring back a case."

Jennifer shook her head. "No, one six-pack is enough. I don't want anyone getting drunk."

Franklin waved his hand. "Can't get drunk on beer. You need whiskey for that. And you know, that's not a bad idea." He faced Kevin. "When go out for beer, bring back a bottle or two of the good stuff."

Jennifer looked in the bag to see if there were any cheeseburgers left. "You ate all the cheeseburgers?"

"And they were damn good," Franklin replied. "Why don't we have cheeseburgers?"

"You're having too much fun," Jennifer teased him. "But maybe sometime we can get our heroic firefighters here to come over for a barbecue. Then you can have cheeseburgers."

"Look forward to it," David said. "In the meantime, can you tell us what that black kid wanted?"

Jennifer walked around the table and pulled up a chair to sit next to William. Susan, who was on the other side, made sure Jennifer could see she wasn't pleased with the seating arrangement. "That kid is

Smokey. He's mixed up with something, something dangerous. He said he needed to notebook I took from him to exchange for his grandmother, who is being held hostage by the owner of the notebook."

William placed his beer on the table. "You didn't give it to him, did you?"

"Yes, I did," Jennifer replied before taking a sip of her beer. "But I made a copy of the entire notebook and two extra pages. I told Smokey to be sure to tell whoever he gave the notebook to that there were copies and that if anything happened to him or his grandmother, the copies would be sent to the police."

William groaned and threw his head back. "Do you know what you just did? You made yourself and the people here targets for these criminals."

Jennifer took another sip of her beer. "I know. And I'm hoping they will come here to get the copies."

"Well, let them come," Franklin blurted out. "They came here once and we chased them off. If they come again, we'll do the same."

Jennifer patted Franklin's hand. "I have a better idea. Why don't we set a trap for them and catch ourselves a killer?'

Franklin smiled and raised his beer. Jennifer and the firefighters raised theirs in agreement.

CHAPTER FORTY-NINE

The knock on the door startled the two men working for the Accountant. They both pulled out their pistols. One of them took a position against a wall while the other one approached the door. The Accountant signaled for them to wait. He didn't like unannounced visitors. There was a second knock on the door. Still, the Accountant signaled for his compatriots to wait. A minute later, the Accountant's phone rang. He answered it. He then motioned for the man at the door to open it.

Smokey stumbled in. "I need your help," Smokey pleaded. "JJ and Theo have my grandmother."

The Accountant sighed. "Why should I care about your grandmother?"

Smokey pulled out the green notebook. "Theo and JJ want this notebook. If I don't get it to them before midnight, they will kill my grandma. But I don't trust them."

The Accountant chucked. "You've got good reason to. I know these two. They aren't known for being trustworthy. These are two people Haj hired to chase you down to get that notebook?"

"Yeah, that's them," Smokey answered.

The Accountant held out his hand. "Let me see the notebook."

Smokey gave it to the Accountant. He opened it. After several minutes, the Accountant closed the notebook. "You told me this is some kind of ledger, but I can't figure it out. It doesn't make sense to me. Are you sure this is Haj's ledger?"

"No, it was my friend's.," Smokey replied.

"What can you tell me about this ledger." Do you know what these entries mean?"

Smokey shook his head. "I can't. But I do know someone who can. Does that help?"

The Accountant tossed the ledger on his desk. "Not unless that person is with you." The room remained silent for several minutes. "Don't stand there. Talk."

Smokey removed two pages from his pockets and placed the pages on the Accountant's desk. "One of the people from this old age home found the ledger. Another one was able to figure out what the numbers mean. They made a copy of the ledger. They said it was for insurance to keep JJ and Theo from killing me and my grandma."

The Accountant grunted. "Let me get this straight. This ledger is in code, which you don't know. But someone else has a copy of it and does know the code. So, you brought the book to me instead of JJ and Theo, who have your grandmother. And if you bring this book to them, they will release her and let you go. And these two are working for Haj, who really wants this book. But you have no idea why this book is so important."

Smokey looked around the room, taking note of the Accountant's two henchmen. "Well, yeah."

"Really?" The Accountant questioned.

"Okay. I mean I know it's some kind of record of the money he collected. But when it was collected and what he did with the money, I don't know."

The Accountant tapped the ledger. "I do. And I'm not going to let you give it to those two clowns working for Haj. You must have known that. So, what do you want me to do?"

Smokey straightened up, standing tall. "I need you to call Haj. Get him to make JJ and Theo to let my grandma go. She's an old lady, and her health is that good."

"Why didn't you call Haj and ask him to get those two guys to let her go? You had the ledger. You knew Haj wanted it. Why not give it to him?"

"Do you know Denise Linden?" Smokey asked.

The Accountant shook his head.

"She was my friend. She was the one who made the notebook. I'm sure Haj killed her to get it. I'm not about to give it to him after he killed my friend."

"You sure he killed her?"

Smokey nodded. "Yeah, I'm sure. Also, about a month ago, someone else I know disappeared."

The Accountant motioned with his hand. "I think I know who you're talking about. Her name was Nancy something."

"Nancy Graham. Sometimes I helped her with collections. She was a friend of Denise's."

"And you think Haj killed her too."

"I have no proof," Smokey replied. "But I'm sure of it. I think the ledger is Denise's way of getting back at Haj."

The Accountant stood up and walked around his desk. He stopped in front of Smokey. "You know I like you. You've never given me any trouble. I even lent you money to get a hotel room. So, I'll let you know what I think is so important about this ledger. It shows the money collected, and I'll bet it shows how much money he gave me to clean for him. If the police ever figure out what the entries mean, I'll go to prison along with Haj and anyone else in there. Now the problem is what to do. You said there was someone at this old age home who decoded this ledger. Who is it? You also said this person had a copy of the ledger. Can you get it from this person?"

"No," Smokey said shaking his head. "They know me and know how interested I am in the ledger and the copy. They won't let me back into the place."

The Accountant nodded that he understood.

"But my grandma," Smokey pleaded. "Can you help me. Maybe you can get Haj to call off JJ and Theo."

The Accountant gave Smokey a slight nod. "Okay. I'll get Haj's goons to turn your grandmother over to me. I'll keep her safe. But I'm going to need you to do me a favor in return. I need you to get the copy of this ledger. Take this JJ and Theo with you. But get that copy."

"What about killing that old man?" Smokey queried.

"What old man?" the Accountant questioned.

"This whole mess started because an old man at that home saw Haj kill Denise. He wants JJ and Theo to kill him. Can't have any witnesses."

"That old man is Haj's problem. I'm only interested in the copy of the ledger. Understand?"

"Yeah," Smokey answered. "Besides, after what he did to Denise, I don't really care what happens to him."

"Good," the Accountant replied. " Get out of here and get a cup of coffee or something. Come back in an hour. Then you and Haj's goons can go get what I want."

One of the henchmen opened the door and motioned for Smokey to leave.

CHAPTER FIFTY
(day fifteen)

A white paper bag startled Stanford as it plopped on his desk. He looked up to see Cat coming into the office. Stanford flicked the bag twice to see if it moved. "Is there something in there that's alive? It's not going to bite me, is it?"

Cat chuckled as she sat down at her desk. "It's breakfast."

"Breakfast?"

"Yes, breakfast," Cat replied. "I got you a bagel with cream cheese and a banana."

Stanford hesitantly picked up the bag and opened it. "Thanks, but I already had breakfast."

"No, you didn't. You had a cup of coffee from the break room and two donuts. Knowing you, they were both frosted."

"What's wrong with donuts?"

From a large shopping bag, Cat pulled out a second white paper bag, opening it to reveal two cups of coffee and a muffin. She passed one of the coffees to Stanford. "I can't believe your wife lets you eat the crap you do. You really do need to improve your diet."

"Me?" Stanford bellowed. "What about you? You're eating a muffin. What do you feed your kid? I'll bet it's takeout and pizza six nights a week."

Cat smirked. "You forget my mother lives with my husband, daughter, and me. Take a guess who does the shopping and the cooking?"

"Okay, okay," Stanford replied as he took a bite of the bagel. "Now that you're here. Let's focus on the case."

Cat raised her coffee in a mock toast. "We have a dead girl, beaten to death in the parking lot of Barnyard Barbecue. We have a witness, who is a really nice guy, but the only thing he could tell us about the killer was he was a white guy with weird ears. Then there is the break-in at the old folks' home. We are fairly certain that the people who did it are our friend Smokey, along with JJ and Theo. But we have no real proof of that. The one person who could identify the perpetrators was the cleaning lady who was shot the next day. She's currently in the hospital in critical condition. Meanwhile, Smokey has disappeared."

Stanford stopped munching on his bagel. "What gets me is why. Why did someone kill that girl at Barnyard Barbecue? What was the motive."

"It wasn't planned," Cat stated. "Who plans to kill a waitress at a restaurant by beating her in a parking lot. It's obvious that he killed her because of some argument."

That means our victim probably had something the killer wanted and she didn't give it to him. Whether he got her to give it up or not is unknown."

Cat shook her head. "I don't think he got what he was after, but that's just a hunch. What I don't understand is how JJ and Theo knew about our witness?"

"Smokey," Stanford said as he finished his bagel. "Smokey was only one outside of the folks at that place who knew about our witness."

Cat put down her coffee. "And the last people to see Smokey were the folks at that home. You know what that means?"

"Yeah. As soon as you finish your muffin, we're going back there."

CHAPTER FIFTY-ONE

William was the first person to notice Stanford and Cat entering Comfort Cottages. He knew they were police officers. Before they could say anything, William immediately went to see Jennifer. He found her in the rec room.

"William, what's up?" Jennifer asked.

"He's here to tell you that we're here," Stanford said as he and Cat joined William and Jennifer. Jennifer reached for William's hand as she faced Stanford.

Cat stepped in front of Stanford. "I hope it won't be an inconvenience, but we would like to talk to the people here who saw Smokey at the funeral, especially Mr. Bolen."

"Why?" Jennifer queried. "You've already talked to them."

"I know," Cat said. "However, we're trying to locate Smokey. And we're hoping Mr. Bolen can give us some more information about the homicide that took place a couple of weeks ago."

Jennifer let go of William's hand before facing Stanford and Cat. "I think we should get some coffee. Then go to my office."

"Sounds like a good idea," Stanford said before Cat could object."

The three of them went to the dining room and got a cup of coffee. Stanford also snatched a muffin. Jennifer led them to her office. Once they were inside, she closed the door.

"I'm a bit concerned about why you want to find Smokey," Jennifer stated.

Stanford raised his muffin to signal he understood Jennifer's concern. "We know Smokey didn't kill Denise Linden. We also believe he's not responsible for the break-in or the shooting that took place here. But we're fairly certain that he does know who did kill Ms. Linden and who did shoot your employee. I need to stress as far as we can tell, he hasn't committed any crime and he's not in trouble, least not with us."

Jennifer stared at the two detectives before taking a sip of her coffee. She placed her cup on her desk and folded her hands, placing them on the desk. "I'm very concerned about Smokey. Yesterday, he came here and informed me that his grandmother had been taken hostage to force him to steal a notebook from us."

"Notebook? What notebook?" Cat asked.

"When our residents went to the woman's funeral and saw Smokey, they also found a notebook," Jennifer explained. "It was basically a bunch of numbers. One of our residents used to be an accountant. She thought it might be a ledger of some kind. She kept it and worked on it. She was finally able to figure most of it out."

"Where's this notebook now?" Cat asked.

"I gave it to Smokey," Jennifer answered. "He needed to trade it for his grandmother."

"Crap," Stanford blurted out. "Do you realize that once whoever had his grandmother would kill him and her once he got the notebook? They're probably dead. And who knows when we'll find the bodies."

"I don't think so," Jennifer firmly stated. "I made a copy of the notebook and made sure Smokey knew I had it. It was insurance that he and his grandmother would be released unharmed. I even gave him two pages that I copied as proof that it existed."

"Where's this copy?" Stanford demanded.

"Safe," Jennifer declared. "And until I see Smokey and his grandmother, it will remain where it is."

Cat put up her hands to calm Stanford. "Do you know where they are?"

Jennifer shook her head. "No."

Cat leaned forward. "Look, I know you think you're helping Smokey. But you're not. We need to find him, and this notebook. It's probably the evidence we need to put the killer behind bars."

"I understand," Jennifer acknowledged. "But keeping the copy I have hidden is the best way I can think of to keep Smokey safe."

Stanford stood up and motioned to Cat they were leaving. 'You're mistaken," he said. "The only thing you've done is put more people in danger. The person who killed Denise Linden won't hesitate to kill you or anyone who stands in his way of getting that ledger."

Jennifer smiled at the detectives. "I'm aware of that. And I'm prepared for it."

CHAPTER FIFTY-TWO

The air whooshed out of the vinal cushion of the easy chair as one of the Accountant's henchmen sat down. "This is nice," he said.

Ms. Simpson sneered at the henchman as she sat down at her kitchen table. Smokey reached across to touch her hand. "Grandma, just relax. No sense in getting upset."

"Why shouldn't I be upset," she snapped. "First, those two goons kidnap me and drag me to some old, cold factory and threaten me. Now these other two goons are keeping me prisoner in my own home. And forcing you to help those others steal something; and that something is going to get you thrown in jail." She leaned forward and whispered, "That is if they don't kill us first."

Smokey glanced over at the henchman in the chair before he murmured to his grandmother, "Calm down. This guy is here to keep us safe. He'll make sure JJ and Theo won't bother us."

"What are you two whispering about over there?" the henchman asked.

"What's it to you?" Simpson replied as she held her head high, showing defiance.

The chair squeaked as the henchman stood up and approached the grandmother. "Listen lady, I don't want any hassles. All I have to do is keep you safe until this mess is over. I don't want any trouble. I would hate to hurt you."

"You won't get any trouble from us," Smokey replied. "I'm just glad the Accountant got JJ and Theo to let me and my grandma go."

"Don't forget your part in this," the henchman responded. "You need to help those two get the copy of the ledger and key to understanding it."

"What happens after that?" Simpson asked with hostility in her voice.

The henchman took a deep breath. "Again, I'm here to keep you safe. All we need is for Smokey to do his part, that's all."

The conversation was interrupted by the tone of a cell phone ringing. The henchman pulled it out of his pocket. He turned his back to Smokey and his grandmother. He took several steps to separate himself. Neither Smokey nor his grandmother could hear any part of the conversation except for the grunts of acknowledgment from the henchman. The conversation ended when the henchman closed his cell phone. He turned to face Smokey.

"That was the Accountant. He said you're to meet JJ and Theo at the restaurant where the girl was killed. You meet them at nine o'clock tonight."

Smokey looked at his grandmother before nodding to the henchman. "Do they have a plan? It's not like we can walk in there and ask for the copy of the ledger."

The henchman shrugged his shoulders. "Don't know what they have planned. All I know is you have to be there."

CHAPTER FIFTY-THREE

Melissa sat at one of the dining room tables with Brenda, Joseph, and Dot. Melissa picked up a pencil and started tapping a pad of blank paper with it. "You all saw the detectives who came here earlier. They want that ledger that Dot worked on."

"What are we going to do?" Joseph asked. "The police are handling it."

Melissa held the pencil up to signal for everyone to be quiet. She leaned over to look around the others at the table. She straightened up. "Brenda's grandson and a couple of his buddies have been hanging around here for several days. They are here for one reason, and one reason only. We're in danger and they want to protect us."

"Well, my grandson can," Brenda adamantly stated. "He and his friends are firemen. They face danger every day."

Melissa exhaled. "Yes, your grandson and his friends are heroes. I admire what they do on a daily basis. But they are no match for a person with a pistol. Let's face it. If we are going to stop whoever is after that ledger, we need to be smarter. We certainly can't overpower them, so, we need to outsmart them."

"And how to you suggest we do that?" Brenda snidely asked.

"We set a trap," Melissa answered.

∞∞∞∞∞∞

Stanford was humming *Sitting on the Dock of the Bay.* Cat smiled and leaned back in the passenger seat of the car. "Sitting in the car in the parking lot," she sang to the tune Stanford was humming.

Stanford stopped his humming. "I take it you disapprove of the places I take you."

"It's a good thing this isn't a date," Cat murmured. "This place is losing its appeal."

"Hey, we're on a stake out. I'm sure whoever is after Smokey, is also after the copy."

"So, we're here in Comfort Cottages parking lot hoping whoever is after the copy will show up and we can stop them before they can get it or hurt anyone. What about the firemen who are hanging out here protecting the residents?"

"We'll worry about that when the time comes."

∞∞∞∞∞

Standing in the parking lot of Barnyard Barbecue, Smokey looked at his cell phone to get the time. He had thirty minutes before he had to meet JJ and Theo. He wasn't ready to go in and wait for them. He looked up at the rear of Comfort Cottages. The wall and the fence were the only barriers separating the parking lot from the facility. Smokey backed up several paces, took several deep breaths, and ran full tilt at the wall. His right foot hit the wall, which he used to propel himself to the top of the wall. He grabbed the top of the wall and managed to pull himself up. Once on top of the wall, Smokey took a few steps to the fence, which he easily climbed over. He faced the back of the facility. Staying low, he made his way to the front of Comfort Cottages. He crouched down behind a bush to watch the parking lot.

Until now, Smokey never gave much thought to the noises of the night. He could hear the crickets, leaves rustling in the wind, even the sound of a small animal, probably a cat, walking through the yard. His eyes adjusted to the dark and the shadows began to take shape. Then a car's headlights ruined his night vision and the engine noise drowned out the sounds of the night. The car stopped and a man got out. He pulled out of his car a case of beer and two plastic bags. He closed the door of his car, turned, and nodded to another car in the parking lot. There was movement from inside of that car. Smokey slowly backed away from the bush, making his way toward the back of the building. He stopped to listen for any sounds of someone following him. There were none. Smokey quickly climbed the fence and jumped down from the wall. He pulled out his cell phone and discovered it was time to meet JJ and Theo.

CHAPTER FIFTY-FOUR

Valerie stopped breathing when JJ and Theo walked into Barnyard Barbecue. The two men found an empty table and sat down. Valerie took a deep breath. She watched the two men as she made her way to the kitchen. She waved one of the other waitresses over. "I need your help," she pleaded. "Could you cover for me. I need to get out of here."

"Is there a problem?" the other waitress asked.

Valerie looked around to see if anyone in the kitchen was watching. "No, no problem," Valerie answered. "I just need to see someone. It's kind of important and it can't wait."

"Got you covered," her coworker said, patting Valerie on her arm.

∞∞∞∞∞∞

Smokey walked around the parking lot, wiping his hands on his trousers. He approached the entrance to the restaurant. Through the window he saw JJ and Theo sitting at a table. He reached for the door handle when he heard footsteps in the parking lot. Smokey took a few steps back and saw a woman running to her car. He retraced his steps to the door and stepped inside. He remained by the door, looking out as the woman in the car drove out of the parking lot. He left the entrance to keep his appointment with JJ and Theo.

"It's about time you got here," JJ said as Smokey approached him and Theo.

Smokey sat down. He remained silent, staring at the two men who tormented his grandmother.

JJ leaned over and tapped the table with his forefinger. "You're lucky Haj called and told us to let your grandmother go. He said you had the notebook, but you gave it to the Accountant. Not cool."

"I know," Smokey replied. "But let's not kid ourselves. If I had given you the notebook, you would have killed me and my grandma. So, I really had no choice."

"Well, you better deliver tonight," JJ hissed. "The Accountant said there was a copy and someone figured out the code for the notebook. If we don't get them, you may still meet with an unpleasant end." To reinforce the point, Theo grinned and made a pistol with his thumb and forefinger, which he pointed at Smokey.

The discussion was interrupted when a waitress came over. Smokey waited till she gave them menus and took their drink orders before he turned his attention to JJ and Theo.

Smokey picked up his menu. "I can recommend the brisket barbecue. I've had it before and it's really good. Also, try their potato salad; it's great."

"We ain't here to eat," Theo replied. "We're here to get that copy of the notebook."

Smokey put down his menu and stared at the two men. "Then you're going to be disappointed."

Theo reached across the table. JJ grabbed Theo's arm and motioned for him to sit down. JJ turned to face Smokey. "Either we get that copy, or we're taking you to Haj. And he's not too happy with you at the moment."

"Listen," Smokey started to explain. "The copy of the notebook is up there at that old folks' home behind here. It's sitting in a desk in the manager's office. But here's the problem. Sitting in the parking lot are two cops. Inside the building are several others. I think they're related to some of the residents. What this means is if we go in after that copy, we'll get picked up by the cops, the copy goes to them, and the woman who knows how to decode the stuff will tell them everything. So, my suggestion is to enjoy dinner and think of another way to get in there without anyone knowing."

Theo and JJ leaned back in their chairs. Smokey pointed the waitress who was returning with their drinks.

"Ready to order?" she asked.

Smokey handed her the menu. "Beef brisket with potato salad and cole slaw." He motioned to JJ and Theo. "What about you guys?"

"We'll have the same," JJ answered, grabbing the menu from Theo, and handing both menus to the waitress. "We'll have the same sides."

"Good choice," the waitress replied as she took the menus. "It'll take a few minutes, but the brisket is worth the wait." She smiled as she turned and left.

Theo waited until she was out of sight. "All right, smart guy. What do you recommend? Haj and the Accountant want that copy."

"Well, I can't go in there," Smokey answered. "It'll be a red flag for the cops to come and arrest us. Sneaking in out of the question. There are people in there waiting for us."

"I didn't ask what we can't do," Theo said as he leaned closer to Smokey. "We need to know what we can do. Do you have a plan?"

Smokey gave Theo a slight nod. "Maybe. I'll tell you my idea after we eat."

CHAPTER FIFTY-FIVE

Cat was the first one to notice a car pulling into the parking lot of Comfort Cottages. "I see it," Stanford said. "Let's see who it is."

They watched as a young lady got out of the car and went into the facility. "Isn't that the waitress we talked to at Barnyard Barbecue?" Cat asked.

"Yeah, it is. Wonder why she's here."

∞∞∞∞∞∞

Valerie stopped inside the entrance to Comfort Cottages. She looked around, hoping to find someone she recognized. She took a few steps forward before stopping again. A young black man came out of an office and approached her.

"Thought I heard someone come in," the man said. "How can I help you?"

"Are you a patient here?" Valerie asked.

"No," the man giggled. "I'm the night attendant here. Are you here to visit one of the residents?"

Valerie let out a sigh of relief. "I'm a friend of Denise Linden. She was killed a couple of weeks ago. At her funeral, I met some people from here. I was hoping I could talk to some of them."

"Do you know their names?"

"Sorry, no, I don't. I remember one lady was in a wheelchair and one of the other ladies was dressed in really nice and kind of expensive clothes.

Leroy nodded. "Probably Melissa Kelsey and Dot. Dot uses a wheelchair."

"Can I see them?" Valerie asked.

"I'll get Melissa, and the person you described. Her name is Dorothy Fletcher." Leroy motioned for Valerie to remain in the foyer before leaving her.

A few minutes later, Leroy returned and nodded to Valerie letting her know the women she was waiting for would soon join her. Valerie watched as Leroy returned to his desk.

She was staring at Leroy when a voice from behind startled her. Valerie turned on her heels, barely able to keep her balance, to find Dot in her wheelchair. Melissa was entering the foyer a few feet behind Dot.

"This is a pleasant surprise," Melissa said as she joined Dot. "What can we do for you?"

Valerie took a quick glance at Leroy, hoping he wasn't watching them. She saw that he was. She stepped a bit closer to Melissa and Dot so that she could lower her voice. "Remember the other day at the funeral? We saw Smokey being chased by two guys."

Both Dot and Melissa acknowledged they did.

"Well, I just saw those two guys at Barnyard Barbecue. I don't think they came in for dinner. I don't know why, but I think they are going to do something, and I think they may be after Smokey. I don't know who to talk to. But I've got to warn him."

Melissa stepped forward and took Valerie's hand to calm her. "I'm sure you're right. Smokey was here yesterday to get a notebook. Our manager, Jennifer, gave it to him; but she made a copy of it."

"A green notebook, with lots of numbers?"

"That's right," Dot answered. "It was some kind of ledger, in code. Well, maybe not a code, but it was written in such a way that most people couldn't understand it. But I was able to figure it out. As Melissa said, Jennifer made a copy as a form of insurance. We're not sure why Smokey was in danger, but you are correct. He is."

Melissa was still holding Valerie's hand so Valeries clasped their hands with her free hand. "Can you warn Smokey?"

Dot faced Valerie and Melissa. "Were they a big guy and a smaller one. I'll bet they're the same ones who broke into here and tried to kidnap Franklin."

Valerie released Melissa's hand. "If that's the case," Melissa replied. "They may be planning to break into here again. This time for the copy Jennifer has and for Franklin."

"Let them try," Leroy shouted from his desk. "This time we're ready for them."

Valerie looked around at all three of them. "I doubt it. I'm sure this time they will come prepared for resistance."

CHAPTER FIFTY-SIX

It should have been romantic. Here Jennifer was sitting in a chair next to William, just the two of them in the dark. Jennifer reached over and clasped William's hand. He returned the gesture. Although William couldn't see it, he was sure Jennifer was smiling. "Kind of a strange way to spend the evening," William stated. "Here we are sitting in the dark in your office, waiting for someone to sneak in and steal the copy of that ledger you made."

Jennifer reached over with her other hand and squeezed William's arm as she placed her head on his shoulder. "I don't mind. I like hanging out with you."

William turned his head and gently kissed the top of Jennifer's head. "I like it too."

Jennifer took her head off his shoulder and stretched up to kiss him. Her phone rang interrupting the moment. Jennifer let out a sigh as she pulled her phone from her jeans. "This had better be good," She demanded. "You're interrupting a very important stake out."

Leroy was on the other end of the phone conversation. "Then get ready. A waitress from that restaurant behind us just came in. She told us two guys are down there planning something. They may be coming up here to grab that copy you made of the ledger."

"Thanks for the warning."

"You still with that fireman?"

Jennifer smiled as she squeezed William's hand. "Yeah, he's still here. We're sitting in the dark trying to lure our burglar into our trap. How about the other two? Where are they?"

"They're in the rec room," Leroy replied. "I've arranged a signal. I'll send them a text on my cell phone as soon as I suspect something. One of them came in earlier and said there were two cops outside in the parking lot."

"Yeah, I know," Jennifer acknowledged. "They told us they would be there. It's a good thing too. If there's any trouble, they can handle it."

"So, we just wait until they come here to steal the copy?" William said.

Jennifer placed her phone on her desk before reaching over to touch William's face. "Well, we could something more than waiting."

∞∞∞∞∞∞

Shadows concealed the three individuals as they snuck to the rear of Comfort Cottages. Smokey cringed as he heard each step JJ and Theo took. Even their breathing disrupted the quiet. Smokey stopped the other two as they approached the back door.

"Listen," Smokey said, "this will only work if you are quiet."

"We are quiet," JJ hissed.

Smokey patted the air with his palms. "Try to breathe easier."

"Breathe easier," Theo huffed. "You're the one who made us climb that wall and fence. It's not our fault we're out of breath. Besides, who's going to hear us out here?"

Smokey again motioned with his palms for JJ and Theo to be quiet. He moved along the side of the building, ducking below the windows. JJ and Theo followed Smokey and his behavior. The three of them stopped at the corner of the building where they could observe the parking lot.

Smokey pointed to a couple of shadows in a car. "See the two cops in that car? And there are a couple of firemen inside waiting. Now, do you understand why we can't get the copy tonight?"

"How did you know?" Theo asked.

"I saw one of the waitresses at the restaurant leave just before I met you," Smokey answered. "She was a friend of Denise's. You remember Denise, the woman Haj killed. Also, I came up here earlier and saw the cops and some others go into the building."

JJ let out a deep breath. "So, what do you suggest we do? We need to get that copy and the code to decipher the ledger."

"Don't forget we still have to take care of that old man," Theo added. "Maybe we could do that tonight?"

"Bad idea," Smokey whispered. "If you kill him, they will probably send the copy and the person who deciphered it to the cops. No, it's better to get the stuff first. As for that old man, he probably won't remember anything. Haj really has nothing to worry about."

"You're probably right, but we still have to get that copy," JJ insisted in a low whisper. "So, do you have a plan?"

Even in the dark, JJ could see Smokey glaring at him, "Yeah, I have a plan, but it will have to wait until tomorrow."

CHAPTER FIFTY-SEVEN
(day sixteen)

"Coffee ready?" William asked.

"Hey, good morning to you too," Jennifer replied. "You know you weren't the only one up all last night."

"That reminds me," William said, holding an empty cup and watching the coffee machine. "Where is the woman who told us Smokey and his buddies were coming last night?"

"She with those two detectives. What about your friends?"

"They're flaked out, grabbing some z's."

Jennifer placed her hand on William's chest, walking her fingers up to his chin. "Next time we spend the night together, let it not be on a stakeout."

William set his coffee cup on the counter and reached for Jennifer. "There you are," a voice interrupted the moment. William reached up and removed Jennifer's arms from his neck.

He faced the voice. "Susan, you're here early."

"I knew Jennifer was working late last night. I figured she would be coming in late, so I thought I should come in early. By the way, do you mind if I have some coffee?"

With an exasperated response, Jennifer poured Susan a cup. "Glad you're here. William and I were on a stake out all last night. We heard someone might try to break in and cause some trouble."

"Oh, my goodness," Susan exclaimed as she moved next to William and grabbed his arm. "You, poor dear. I bet you're dead on your feet."

"Yeah, Jennifer and I spent the night in her office waiting for the thief," William replied.

Susan let go of William's arm and took a step away from him. "Why there was no reason for you to be here. There were a couple of cops watching the place. And, we had Leroy here. If anyone broke in, I'm sure he would call the police."

"We know," William said as he reached for a coffee cup.

"No," Susan commanded. "The last thing you need is coffee. Now come with me and I'll show you where we set up a room for you and your friends can get some sleep." Susan faced Jennifer. "Why don't you go home and take the day off? I have everything covered here. Just go home and I'll take care of William."

Jennifer crossed her arms and coldly replied while glaring at Susan. "Thanks. Maybe I'll take your suggestion."

"In that case," Susan said as she grabbed William's arm, "I'll see you tomorrow."

Jennifer watched as Susan dragged a reluctant William down the hall to join his friends. Melissa passed them as she entered the dining room. She joined Jennifer next to the coffee machine. Melissa pointed toward Susan. "There are times when I think that girl is so dumb that it would take her three guesses which way an elevator is going, and the worst thing is, she's on the ground floor."

"She's not stupid," Jennifer argued. "She's as determine as a starving dog after bacon."

Melissa poured herself a cup of coffee. "Bacon isn't kosher. Maybe she should try going after another fireman"

"She can chase a pig for all I care."

Melissa poured a second cup of coffee and gave it to Jennifer. "Don't worry dear. She can try all she wants, but that man is going to let only one woman catch him. And we both know it's not going to be Susan."

Jennifer took a couple of sips of her coffee. "Still, she's right. I should go home and get some sleep. William let me grab a cat nap during the night, but I am dead tired."

Now, you can appreciate Leroy and what he does when he is the night attendant," Melissa said, holding up her cup in an imaginary toast to Leroy.

Jennifer put down her coffee. "Listen, I am going home. Please do me a favor. If anything out of the ordinary happens, call me. I locked my desk and my office, so no one should be in there. But just because nothing happened last night, that doesn't mean we're not in danger of someone coming in and trying something. Now that it's daylight, the cops that were watching the place have gone and our heroes are asleep. So, be alert and be careful."

"There's an old saying," Melissa said, holding her head high. "I didn't get to be this old without learning to take care of myself. And, we all have lots of tricks up our sleeves."

∞∞∞∞∞∞

Smokey could tell JJ and Theo were frustrated. The three of them were sitting in a van, waiting in the parking lot of Barnyard Barbecue. "What are we doing here?" JJ asked. "Last night was a waste, and now, we've spent the entire day just waiting. It's almost time for dinner. So, just what are we doing here?"

Smokey gave JJ a disapproving look. "We didn't waste last night. They were waiting for us, and I did you a favor by warning you about the cops and the others. As for wasting the day, it's only four o'clock. What we're doing is waiting for someone. Once she shows up, I need you two to stay in the car. I'll take care of everything."

JJ snorted. "What's your plan? You going to kidnap someone in broad daylight? We have enough people to deal with. We don't need any more."

Smokey continued to stare at JJ. "The problem with you and Theo is you solve problems with violence. I have a plan, and it doesn't involve hurting anyone. Just stay in the car and let me talk to the person we're waiting for. Do it my way, and no one gets hurt."

"We need that copy of the ledger and the code," Theo interjected. "I don't see how talking to someone here is going to help us."

"Just do what I ask, "Smokey said. "You'll find out what you need to know when the time is right."

"When's that?" JJ demanded.

Smokey held up his hand to signal for JJ and Theo to be quiet. "Right now. See that woman who just got out of her car. She's the person we've been waiting for."

Smokey waited until Valerie entered the restaurant. He got out of his car and slowly walked over to the door. He stopped and looked to ensure JJ and Theo remained in the car.

He entered the restaurant and found an empty table. A few minutes later, Valerie entered the dining room to begin her shift. Smokey got up. "Hi. Do you remember me?" Smokey asked as he approached her.

Valerie let out a small yelp as she turned to face Smokey. "You surprised me."

"Sorry about that. You know I was Denise's friend, and I kind of need your help."

Valerie took a step back and brought her hands to her chest. "I saw you at Denise's funeral. Some guys were chasing you. I don't know what you're mixed up in, but I don't want to get involved."

Smokey wiped his hand down his face and looked around. "It's okay. All I need is for you to help me get in touch with the people from the old folks' home. You know, the ones that came to Denise's funeral."

"Why?"

Smokey again looked around. "I think they may be in danger. Remember those guys who chased me. I think the people at that place may have something they want. I've got to warn them."

"I was there last night. They know about those guys. They even have the police staking out the place. In fact, last night, they were waiting for those guys to come there and try something."

"That's great," Smokey said. "Still, I really do need to talk to them. Do you think you could help me?"

"How?"

Smokey pulled out a piece of paper. "Here's my phone number. Have one of them call me. That way I can arrange to meet them and give them information on the guys that chased me. I would really appreciate it."

Valerie tentatively took the note from Smokey. "That's all? Just have them call you?"

Smokey held up his hands. "That's it. Just need to let them know who they are up against. I'm just trying to help."

Valerie nodded her head before she turned and walked away. Smokey smiled as he left the restaurant.

∞∞∞∞∞

Valerie stepped into the manager's office and pulled out the note with Melissa's information on it. She picked up the phone and dialed the number. Melissa answered and Valerie gave her Smokey's message.

CHAPTER FIFTY-EIGHT

The alarm from his cell phone woke Stanford. He stretched his arms and lifted the cat from his lap as he got up from his recliner and turned off the television. He pushed the icon to the side to answer the incoming call. "It's your dime. Tell me what you want."

"I want to realize this is the twenty-first century and phone calls now cost more than ten cents," the voice at the other end stated.

"Cat, it's too early to call. I need coffee." Stanford heard Cat snicker on the other end.

"It's almost five," Cat said. "Are we going to stake out the assisted living facility again tonight?"

"Do you want to?"

"No," Cat emphatically stated. "I want to spend the evening with my husband, who is getting jealous of all the time I'm spending with you, and I want to spend it with my daughter, who is beginning to think I'm a stranger who shows up every once in a while to shower and sleep."

"Sounds better than my plans," Stanford said trying not to yawn. "I'm planning on sleeping in front of the TV with a cat in my lap."

"That's it?"

"Well, I will wake up when the wife gets home, especially if she brings dinner."

"So, who's going to be on stake out tonight?"

Stanford pulled his phone away from his face as he let out a loud yawn and stretched. He brought the phone back to his mouth. "There are those firemen there. I told them to call us if there is any trouble. Also, I talked to the night attendant. They have enough people there."

Cat groaned. "I'm not sure that's enough. I'm going to see if we can't assign a plains clothes unit to watch the place. The very least, I'm going to have a patrol unit check on the place a couple of times every hour."

"I noticed you're not giving up your free evening."

"Hey, at least I'm not spending it with a cat."

"What, you don't like cats?"

"Good night, Stanford. Hope you have a good night."

"I'm just hoping no one will call."

Cat let out a loud sigh. "You and me both, but I wouldn't count on it."

∞∞∞∞∞∞

The evening meal wasn't for another hour when Melissa got the phone call from Valerie. The request to call Smokey was unusual. She had shared a single meal with him, which was cut short when Freya was shot. However, seeing Smokey being chased by two men, as well as knowing he had been back trying to get the ledger they had found at the funeral, gave Melissa an uneasy feeling, but compelled her to follow Valerie's instructions and call Smokey. She punched in his phone number.

Breathing heavily, he answered on the second ring. "Yeah."

"Is that any way to answer a phone," Melissa criticized. "The least you can do is say 'Hello,' in a polite voice."

"Sorry," Smokey said. "You one of the ladies from the old folks' home?"

"I must apologize. This is Melissa Kelsey. We had dinner once at Comfort Cottages. I received a message that you needed to talk to one of us."

"Oh, yes," Smokey responded in a loud voice. "I need to talk to the lady in the wheelchair. You know, the one who figured out the stuff in the ledger. Can I meet her someplace? Maybe at Barnyard Barbecue? It won't take long."

"Well, I'll have to ask her. When do you want to meet?"

"How about in an hour?"

Melissa walked to the front entrance of Comfort Cottage, checking for any danger lurking in a parked car. She scanned the parking lot, looking for movement. "It's almost time for our evening meal. Couldn't this wait until tomorrow?"

"Kind of in a bind," Smokey answered. "I need to clear up something tonight. Tomorrow I'll be super busy, so I won't be able to meet up with you. And I really don't want to wait too long. Why don't I meet you and the other lady at Barnyard Barbecue and I'll buy you both dinner?"

"Is it really that important?"

"It kind of is."

"I'll see if she's available," Melissa replied. "I'll call you back and let you know if a few minutes." She cut the call and hurried down the hall.

Twenty minutes later, Melissa opened the door as she and Dot exited Comfort Cottages. "Did you call Smokey back?" Dot asked.

"Yes, I did. He said he would meet us there."

Dot pressed the switch to move her wheelchair forward. "Do you really think this is a good idea?"

"Last night, we had the police, Brenda's grandson, and his friends, and several of us waiting for Smokey and friends. If they won't come to us, we'll go to them."

Dot took a deep breath hoping it would give her courage to keep moving forward. "I just hope your idea works."

"So do I," Melissa replied, determined to show confidence in their plan. She hoped it would work. If not, the consequences could be deadly.

∞∞∞∞∞∞

They were at least a hundred yards and out of sight from the entrance to Comfort Cottages. The spot was perfect. The closest house was on the other side of an abandoned house with overgrown bushes. They knew the two ladies would pass this way.

JJ and Theo got out of the van they had borrowed. They opened the back doors and made sure the ramp could be easily pulled out. All they had to do was wait.

CHAPTER FIFTY-NINE

Jennifer stumbled into her office and flopped in the chair behind her desk. She knew she should have stayed home, but her anxiety made it difficult to sleep. She tried to sleep since she left Comfort Cottages that morning. She was able to catch two naps when she was watching television. Jennifer was beginning to question whether coming in was the right decision.

Susan entered the with enthusiasm and a joyous yelp. "Jennifer, you're here. Are we going to do a stake out tonight? William and I can stay in the dining room while Leroy is at his desk. That way we can trap the bad guys."

"What about William's friends, David and Kevin? Aren't they in the dining room with the rest of the residents?"

Susan held up two fingers to her face before answering. "I'll have to check, but they are probably there."

Jennifer let out a soft groan as she moved pass Susan, who followed Jennifer to the dining room. Upon entering, Jennifer waved her hand in the direction of the three firefighters who were sitting with Brenda.

"Good to see you guys here," Jennifer said as she approached their table. "How's the food?"

"You should let Kevin cook," William answered.

"Stop that," Brenda scolded her grandson. "The food is fine. Besides, this is the best they can do. You get to cook for a few people and everyone eats at the same time. Here, they cook for eighty people who come in when they are ready. And don't forget, we're allowed to go out or order in if we want."

William hung his head. "Sorry, I didn't mean to be insulting."

Susan put her hand on William's shoulder. "No need to apologize."

Jennifer moved to the other side of William. "If you have any suggestions on how to improve our dining service, I would love to hear them. We want the best for our residents." Jennifer put her hand on Kevin's shoulder. "And if Kevin wants to come here and cook for us, he's welcome to do so at any time."

"Sorry, but I'm not giving up my day job," Kevin joked.

Jennifer smiled as she looked around the dining room. She saw who was there, but what she noticed most was who wasn't. "Where are Dot and Melissa? Don't they usually eat with you?"

"They left a few minutes ago," William answered. "Said they had an errand to run."

Jennifer took another look around the dining room, unable to hide her anxiety and dread coming from the absence of the two. "Exactly what was this errand they had to run?" Jennifer demanded.

"They didn't say," Brenda stated.

"Okay," Jennifer said slowly before she left the group and headed back to her office. She picked up her cell phone and called Stanford.

∞∞∞∞∞∞

Cat's five-year-old daughter laughed as Cat tickled her. It was a fun game that ended with the ring tone from Cat's cell phone.

"Detective Diaz."

"Oh, good. I got the right number."

"What's up Stanford? We're spending the night in, remember?"

"Just got a call from the manager of the rest home. Two of her people are missing and she's worried."

"So, send a patrol car over there. Have them handle it."

"Already did," Stanford replied. "But she's really worried. And I would hate to find out later that something happened to them and we didn't respond. Sorry, but I think we should check it out. Look, if it's nothing, we can come home and watch TV."

Cat smiled and waved at her daughter before making a claw with her hand and threatening to tickle her again. She withdrew her hand and straightened up. "You're ruining my life, and that of my daughter. I hope you're happy."

"I'm overjoyed. I'll pick you up in a few."

Cat stood up. "I'll be ready. I just have to say good night to my daughter." Cat discontinued the call. She could see the disappointment in her daughter's face.

∞∞∞∞∞∞

Smokey got out of the van and rambled to the back of it. He leaned his shoulder against the van, facing Melissa and Dot as they approached. Hiding behind him and the open doors were JJ and Theo.

"I thought we were going to meet you at the restaurant?" Melissa inquired as a way to ensure she had understood the instructions Smokey had given her.

"Yeah, we were," Smokey answered. "But I had this van and thought why not give you all a lift."

Dot clasped her hands and smiled. "How very kind of you."

Smokey went around to the back of Dot's wheelchair and pushed it forward. "Think nothing of it."

Both women gasped as they rounded the rear of the van to find JJ and Theo standing there. Before anyone could say anything, Theo grabbed Dot's wheelchair from Smokey and pushed her up the ramp. JJ took hold of Melissa and forced her into the back of the van. JJ and Theo jumped in and closed the doors. Smokey returned to the driver's seat and started the van. He waited a few seconds to let a police patrol car go pass them.

"You hooligans are in a lot of trouble," Melissa asserted, squirming in her seat. "Kidnapping is a serious crime."

"Quiet grandma," JJ hissed. "Wouldn't want to hurt you."

Dot tried to maneuver her chair around to face her abductors. She was unsuccessful so she was forced to speak over her shoulder. "What do you want with us? We're two old ladies who have no money. Holding us for ransom is ridiculous. Nobody is going to pay to us back."

JJ moved closer to Dot. "Didn't I say be quiet. You want me to hurt you."

"Hey, hey," Smokey shouted. "There's no need to hurt anyone. Besides, we need them."

Melissa snorted. "Need us? For what? To do your laundry? What can you possibly need from us? You should just let us go. So far, the only thing you're done is scare a couple of old ladies. That's hardly a crime."

Smokey pulled the van over and turned in his seat. "Listen. We need you to help us with something. Once that's done, we'll let you go."

"You need to let us go now," Dot shouted. "If we don't get back home, people will miss us. And they aren't going to let you do anything to hurt us."

JJ moved closer to Dot where he could almost whisper in her ear. "That's what we're counting on."

CHAPTER SIXTY

The patrol car pulled up to the entrance where Jennifer was standing with her arms across her chest. The patrol officer exited his vehicle. "Evening ma'am. You called about a couple of missing people?"

"That's right," Jennifer said and she let out a deep breath. "Two of our residents left to do an errand. I tried calling them on their cell phones, but there was no answer. Because of a couple of recent break-ins here, I'm concerned for their safety. If you follow me into my office, I'll get their information and their photos."

"You have photos of your residents?"

Jennifer glared at the patrol officer. "We have a lot of social events and we take photos at them. I picked out a few photos they were in. But to answer your question, no we don't take mug shots of our residents."

Jennifer led the officer into the building and her office where she handed him photos of the residents at a Christmas party. She also provided information about Melissa and Dot. The presence of the police officer attracted William's attention, along with that of several others. Jennifer noticed a small crowd clustering outside her office. Her frustration and anxiety increased as she saw Susan hanging onto William as Jennifer closed the door to her office.

"Oh, my goodness," Susan whispered to William, clutching his arm tighter. "Something's happened to Dot and Melissa. This is terrible."

William gently removed Susan's hand from his arm. "Don't jump to conclusions. We don't know what's going on."

To add to Susan's state of fear, Stanford and Cat entered the building, making their way to Jennifer's office. "That's it," Susan cried. "They've been murdered."

"Quiet," William commanded in a harsh whisper. "You don't know what's happened and you don't want to start a panic. Fear is contagious. Keep calm. I'm sure Jennifer will tell us everything in a few minutes. Until then, keep your fears to yourself."

As on cue, Jennifer along with Stanford, Cat, and the patrol officers came out of the office. Stanford nodded to the patrol officer who left. He and Cat faced the group in the hall. "Can we help you?" He asked.

Susan looked around at the small group. She turned to Stanford. "What's happened? Have Melissa and Dot been murdered?"

Jennifer stepped forward. "No!" she shouted. "Melissa and Dot went out on an errand. Because of the break-ins, I called the police to check on them. That's all. I tried to call them, but they didn't answer their cell phones. It's probably nothing and I'm worrying about nothing. But I would rather be a nuisance and find them safe than find out they are in trouble and I was too afraid of my self-image to call the police. Now, everyone, I want you to go about your business. If there is any news, I'll be sure to let you know."

The group started to disperse. Brenda came over to William and gave him a hug. "Lose Susan and then come see me," she whispered in his ear.

∞∞∞∞∞∞

Melissa held her head up high, not out of arrogance but because she refused to show JJ or Theo any fear. Fear may be contagious, but so is courage. Dot gained strength and grit from her associate. Dot's cell phone rang, startling everyone in the van.

"Don't answer it," JJ commanded. "Give it here."

Dot took her phone from her handbag and gave it to JJ. He then motioned for Melissa to give him hers. She did so.

Dot phone fell silent, but a moment later Melissa's phone rang. JJ looked at the caller ID. "Why is the old folks' home calling you two?" he asked.

Dot hesitated. "It's dinner time," Melissa answered. "They're just letting us know that dinner is served. When residents don't show up, they call to let us know. We often forget the time, so they remind us."

"Well, you're going to go hungry tonight," Theo said with a small chuckle.

"Hey, hey," Smokey shouted from the driver's seat. "We can get them something later. No need to be mean to them."

"Quiet," JJ demanded. "Just drive the van."

Melissa smoothed her skirt with her hands. "I take it you think you're the person in charge of this little escapade. Can't wait to meet the person who is really in charge."

"What makes you think I'm not the one in charge?" JJ hissed.

Melissa stared at him for a few seconds. "Because if you were, you would have told us what you want from us. No, I'm quite sure we're on our way to meet the boss, who will explain what he needs two old ladies for."

"Think you're pretty smart," JJ replied. He brought out an automatic pistol and put it down beside him.

"You're not going to kill us," Melissa responded. "You wouldn't have gone through the trouble of kidnapping us if you wanted us dead."

JJ picked up the pistol and pointed it at Melissa's foot. "You're right. I can't kill you. But there is nothing that says I can't hurt you. Now be quiet until I tell you otherwise."

Melissa leaned forward. "If you're trying to frighten me with death threats, you're going to have to better than pointing a gun at my foot."

JJ put the gun back in his pocket. "Lady, you're getting on my nerves. And that is not a good thing to do."

∞∞∞∞∞∞

It took William almost ten minutes before he could get free of Susan. Fortunately, Jennifer came to his rescue by instructing Susan to take a head count and ensure everyone else was safe at the facility. David and Kevin walked around the outside of the building, checking the windows and doors. Meanwhile, Leroy checked all the closets and access areas such as the public toilets.

Brenda was reading a mystery novel when William knocked on her door. She got up to let him in.

"What's up?" he asked.

"I'm sure Melissa and Dot have been kidnapped," Brenda answered.

"You seem pretty calm about it. Do you know where they are?"

"No, I don't."

"Well, we have to tell the police. They're in danger."

Brenda picked up her handbag. "Don't worry. We're going to rescue them. And you and your friends are going to help."

CHAPTER SIXTY-ONE

The van pulled into the back of an old factory. Smokey parked the vehicle. JJ and Theo opened the back of the van and pulled out the ramp. Melissa had difficulty exiting the vehicle because of the high bumper. Theo pulled out Dot in her wheelchair.

Melissa turned to Smokey. "I hope you don't bring all of your dates here." It was getting dark, but Melissa could see the embarrassment on Smokey's face.

JJ shoved Melissa's shoulder. "Come on, grandma. Let's move it."

Melissa took a step forward to steady herself before facing JJ. "Don't call me grandma and don't shove. There is no need for such behavior."

JJ put his hand up to give Melissa another shove. She turned on heels, forcing JJ to push empty air. He regained his balance. Melissa was staring at him. "Like I said. There is no need for such behavior."

"Come on guys," Smokey pleaded. "Treat them with some respect. Let's get this over with so that I can take them back to the home."

Smokey led the way into the building. Melissa and Dot followed him with JJ and Theo bringing up the rear. Melissa noticed JJ shut and locked the door they came in from. They moved through a large empty loading area into a hallway leading to several offices. One of them had the door open and a light on. Smokey, along with Melissa and Dot entered the office. JJ and Theo remained in the hallway. Sitting behind a desk was a man with large earlobes due to the large black plastic rings in them.

"Hello, ladies," the individual said. "Glad you could make it."

"Didn't realize we had a choice," Dot replied with a slight tremor in her voice. She hoped he didn't notice it or how scared she was. "Why were we brought here?"

The man spread two sheets of paper on the desk. "I need you to tell me what these numbers mean. That's all."

Melissa stepped forward to look at the sheets. She straightened up and stared at the man. "Who are you? You could at least tell us your name."

"It's better you don't know who I am."

"And why is that?" Dot demanded.

"I'll tell you why," Melissa interjected. "This is the man who killed that poor woman at Barnyard Barbecue. These sheets are copies of the green notebook we worked on. Unless I'm mistaken, that woman he murdered created the notebook and put these numbers in, but it's in a code he can't decipher. That's why he needs us. We have to tell him how to read the numbers."

The man ran his hand over his hair. "Does it really matter who I am. Just tell me how to figure out what these numbers."

Melissa again held her head up. "It matters to me. We know you intend to kill us. So, yes, I do want to know your name. I think it's only fair we know who our killer is."

"What makes you think I want to kill you?" the man asked.

Melissa leaned slightly forward. "We've seen your faces. We can identify you. Kidnapping in a major felony, which means you can't have any witnesses."

"You're pretty smart." Haj leaned back in his chair and stared at the two women. "My name is Haj. Now you have to make a decision. Are we going to do this the easy way, or the hard way?"

"I'm not sure we should do anything he asks," Dot said, this time she couldn't hide the fear in her voice. "If he's going to kill us, anyway, why should we help him?"

Melissa put her hand on Dot's shoulder. "Because if we don't, he'll torture us until we do. And to be quite honest, I don't think either one of us could stand up to it for any length of time."

Haj let out a small laugh. "You are a smart lady. Do it my way, and I'll make sure your death is quick and as painless as possible. If not, then you going to have a very painful last few hours, and a very painful death."

Dot started shaking. Melissa patted Dot's shoulder. "There, there. It's going to be all right." Melissa turned to Haj. "We'll need a computer and a calendar for last year."

"We could let them use a cell phone," Smokey suggested.

"Never," Haj shouted. "They'll send a text message to the police. No, have JJ and Theo get a calendar and bring back a laptop. That way we can watch what they are doing."

∞∞∞∞∞∞

"What are we doing at the emergency call center?" William asked as he escorted Brenda and Jennifer into the facility.

Brenda turned to Jennifer. "Are you sure those two detectives are still at Comfort Cottages. We're going to need them to call the police."

"Yes," A tired and frustrated Jennifer answered. "But, like William said, what are we doing here?"

Brenda smiled. "We're waiting for a signal. A signal that will let us capture a killer and the ones who kidnapped Melissa and Dot."

CHAPTER SIXTY-TWO

"Find anything?" the patrol officer asked Stanford and Cat as they finished their inspection of the grounds surrounding Comfort Cottages.

"No," Stanford answered. "We checked the grounds and circled the building twice. Didn't see any signs of anyone trying to break in. How about you?"

"Been through the neighborhood and checked several streets over," the patrol officer stated.

"Where's the person who called us?" Cat asked. "If she's so concerned, you would think she would be here to see what we've found out."

The patrol officer shrugged his shoulders. Stanford and Cat sighed and went into the building to find Jennifer. To their disappointment, Susan was in Jennifer's office.

"Excuse me," Cat said to Susan. "Could you tell me where is Ms. Stebbins?"

"She left with one of the residents," Susan replied. "But Leroy is here. I'm sure he can help you." She motioned for the detectives to follow her.

Leroy was checking things in the dining room when Susan with the detectives approached him. Leroy stood behind a table and chairs, as if they provided a barrier between him and the police. "What's up?" he asked.

Stanford stopped the three of them, maintaining a small distance between them and Leroy. "I got a call from Ms. Stebbins earlier. She was concerned about a couple of the people who stay here. She said they were missing."

Leroy nodded. "Yeah, Melissa Kelsey and Dorothy Fletcher weren't at dinner tonight. When Jennifer tried calling them, they didn't answer. She's quite worried about them."

"I'm aware of that," Stanford replied. "We had a patrol unit check around the neighborhood, but they didn't see anything. My partner, Detective Diaz, and I looked around the grounds. Again, nothing. Where is Ms. Stebbins?"

"She left with Brenda Elson and her grandson. He's a fireman. They went to the emergency call center. Brenda said they would find Dot and Melissa there."

"Why would these missing women go to the emergency call center?" a surprised Cat inquired.

Leroy shook his head. "I think it's more of Brenda and Jennifer would find some kind of signal or something that would tell them where Dot and Melissa are."

"That's ridiculous," Susan said. "If Jennifer couldn't get them on their cell phones, how is she going to find Melissa and Dot. Is she going to track their cell phones like they do on TV?"

"Well, it's possible," Cat answered. "If they have a track phone app on their cells, then they can be located. But that can be done by anyone who has the app on their phone. There is no need to go the emergency call center."

Leroy fidgeted with the chair in front of him.

"What's going on?" Stanford demanded.

Leroy crossed his arms. "What do you mean?"

Stanford took a step forward. "You seem a bit nervous. You know something."

Leroy let out a heavy breath. "I really don't know what is going on, but I've been around these people long enough to know when they are up to something. Franklin and Joseph are in the rec room waiting like kids for cookies to come out of the oven. And two of the firefighter friends of Brenda's grandson are hanging around."

Stanford smirked as he tapped Cat's arm. "I've got a feeling the answer to this mystery is with those two gentlemen in the rec room. Let's go find them."

"I'll take you to them," Susan volunteered.

"Not necessary," Stanford replied. "I remember where it is."

Cat and Stanford found Joseph and Franklin watching their phone with the intensity of a dog waiting for a bone. "What's up?" Stanford asked the elderly gentlemen.

"Nothing," Joseph retorted. "Why do you ask?"

Cat and Stanford looked around the rec room. The few other residents were watching a game show on the large-screen television. The detectives returned their gaze to Joseph and Franklin. Neither detective said a word.

Joseph returned the detectives' stare. "What do you want? We're not bothering anybody."

Cat pulled up a chair and sat close to Joseph and Franklin. Looking at Joseph, she responded. "There seems to be two women missing. The manager and two others are at the emergency call center. And you two are here, glued to your phones like teenagers. Call it a hunch, but something is up. Now what is it?"

"We don't have to say anything," Joseph adamantly stated. "We've got rights."

"Yes, you do," Cat said, smiling. "But two women may be in danger. Don't you want to help them?"

"Oh, but we are," Franklin blurted. "We're waiting for a phone call and then we'll go rescue them."

Cat sat up taller. "What do you mean you'll rescue them? Tell me what you are planning."

"We don't have to tell you nothing," Joseph answered. "And no dumb broad is going to make me."

Stanford put his hand on Cat's shoulder. "Don't. Don't let him get to you. Remember, they're old and it's easy to really hurt them."

Cat glared up at Stanford, took a deep breath, and faced Joseph. "Don't call me a dumb broad. I don't like it."

"She's right," Stanford interrupted. "It's rude. And trust me, you don't want to be rude to my partner. Now, tell us who is going to call you, and what are you going to do?"

Joseph smirked at the detectives. "What are you going to do? Arrest us for not talking to you."

Cat leaned over and clasped her hand on Joseph's shoulder. "Ever hear of obstruction of justice? If anyone gets hurt, and I mean anyone, because you refuse to cooperate with us, I will take you in and make sure the courts throw the book at you. This attitude of yours is dangerous. Not to you. Not to us. But to others. So, stuff it and tell us what you're up to."

Joseph crossed his arms over his chest.

They had a standoff. After a minute, Stanford stepped over and put his hand on Franklin's shoulder. "You told me you played ball when you were younger."

Franklin looked up at Stanford. "Are we going to a ball game?"

Stanford smiled and gave Franklin's shoulder a little shake. "Not tonight, but soon. But you know, in a ball game, it's a team sport. You have to rely on everyone in the team. There's no room for grandstanding. If one player tries to take over the game, everyone loses. And you know that. We really need to know what is going on."

"Don't tell him," Joseph shouted, gaining the attention of the others in the rec room.

"Quiet!" Cat commanded.

Franklin continued to look at Stanford. "I can't tell. But if you wait, after the we get a phone call, you can come and help us."

"That's if we let you," Joseph said defiantly.

"You're not going to have a choice," Cat answered with just as much defiance.

CHAPTER SIXTY-THREE

Theo gulped down his drink as he stood over Dot as she searched the internet for data. Melissa sat next to Dot, focusing on the computer screen while watching Theo out of the corner of her eye.

Theo belched and waved his drink cup at Dot. "What's taking so long?"

"It's not that easy," Dot said with frustration. "I have to compare two completely different calendars that have months starting on different days. You want this to be accurate, don't you?"

Theo threw the drink cup on the floor. "I'm going to get JJ to watch you two. Don't try anything."

"You mean like getting out of this wheelchair and running away. Wouldn't think of it."

"I'm quite comfortable here, so I'm not going anywhere," Melissa added.

Theo turned his back to the two women. Dot continued to push keys on the computer. Melissa watched Theo as he went to the doorway and called to JJ. She tapped Dot's knee when he turned away and leaned against the doorway. Dot's hand fell to the side of her wheelchair and pushed a small button in the center of a white pennant.

∞∞∞∞∞∞

A signal buzzed in the emergency call center. "Someone's emergency medical alarm just went off," one of the technicians said. She began working on locating where the signal came from. "I'm not getting a response."

"Do you have a location?" Brenda asked as she hovered over the technician.

"Well, yeah," the technician replied. "It's coming from an old shoe factory on Redwood Avenue. But there is no reply to my inquiry about the emergency."

"It's Dot," Brenda exclaimed. "I know it is."

"What's going on?" William demanded. "You made me bring you here; now tell me what is going on."

Brenda took a deep breath. "Smokey called earlier tonight. He wanted to meet Melissa and Dot at a restaurant. We suspected a trap, so we came up with a plan. We would let Smokey take Melissa and Dot. When she got to wherever he was taking her, and when she found out why he wanted her, Dot would activate her emergency medical alarm button. But if it turned out that it wasn't a trap, either Dot or Melissa would call me." Brenda turned to Jennifer. "When you called them and they didn't answer, I knew they had been kidnapped. That's why I insisted we come here. We needed to be here to find out where her signal came from."

William pulled out his cell phone. "I'll call Kevin and David. We'll meet them at the location of the signal."

"I'll send the police," the technician interjected. "Let them take care of this."

William shook his head. "We're firefighters. Trust me. We'll take care of it." He turned and walked away with Jennifer and Brenda hurrying after him. The technician notified the police anyway.

∞∞∞∞∞∞

Stanford stood against a wall while Cat sat in a chair watching both Joseph and Franklin, who were staring at their phones. Joseph did a little jump from his chair when his cell phone rang. "We're here," he yelled into his phone. "Where are they?"

Brenda was on the other end. She gave him the location.

Joseph ended the call. "Come on. I know where they are."

"Not so fast," Stanford commanded. "Tell us where your friends are and what they are planning to do."

"We laid a trap for the killers," Joseph stated, holding his head up with pride. "Dot and Melissa were the bait. When the killers kidnapped them, Dot pushed her emergency medical alarm button, letting the emergency call center know where she was. Brenda, Jennifer, and Brenda's grandson, the fireman, are at the emergency call center. They are going to rescue Dot and Melissa and capture the killers."

Franklin stood up to face Stanford. "Do you want to come along. You can help us catch them."

Stanford put his hand on Franklin's shoulder and faced Joseph. "Tell us where they are."

"Only if you let come with you," Joseph insisted.

"Fine," Cat bellowed. "Now, tell us."

"Dot and Melissa are at an old shoe factory on Redwood Avenue."

Cat pulled out her cell phone as she headed out of the room. She stopped in the doorway and turned toward Joseph and Franklin. "Wait here. We'll be back for you."

CHAPTER SIXTY-FOUR

JJ turned to see Haj coming toward him. "Where's Theo?" he asked.

"I'm here," Theo replied. "What's up?'

Haj walked over to the two women. He stared at them. They stared back. Haj moved behind Dot and looked at the screen. He looked down at Dot. He saw a dim red glow in the center of a round plastic disc. "What's that?" he demanded as he pulled it away from Dot. He turned to show it to JJ and Theo.

"I don't know," JJ said, running his hand over his hair.

Haj looked around. "Where's Smokey?"

Theo pointed behind him with his thumb. "He's watching the van."

"Get him in here."

Theo left. A moment later he returned with Smokey.

Haj held up the plastic disc. "Do you know what this is?"

"Sure," Smokey answered. "My grandma has one. It's an emergency medical alarm button. You press it if you're having a heart attack or fall down and can't get up. Why?"

Haj motioned with his head toward Dot. "She had it."

"Crap," Smokey shouted. "If she pushed the button, then the cops know where we are. They can track us with that."

"Give it here and I'll smash it," Theo said as he reached for it.

"No," Haj argued. "Take these two and load up everything. Now."

Theo grabbed Dot and pushed her away while JJ dragged Melissa with him. Haj grabbed the computer. He cursed having to rush out, but there was no other option.

∞∞∞∞∞∞

"You know, those two are going to be really pissed that you left them behind," Stanford said as he focused on the road ahead of them.

Cat scoffed. "I wasn't about to bring two old men with us while we try to rescue two women, one of them in a wheelchair."

"What about Ms. Stebbins and her firemen friends? What are you going to do about them?"

"I'm hoping the patrol units are there when we arrive. They can take care of our heroes."

Cat looked out the passenger window before facing Stanford. "Do you have a plan? We can't rush in there."

Stanford nodded in agreement. "First, we make sure they are trapped. Then we go in and talk them into surrendering. I'm hoping they will realize the situation and surrender."

"That's it?"

"Well, I'm also hoping no one gets shot, especially us."

∞∞∞∞∞∞

"That wasn't nice of those two cops to leave us back there," Joseph said to Franklin.

"But we'll show them," Franklin replied. "We'll get there and save those two. That will teach those cops that just because we're old, it doesn't mean we can't take out a couple of crooks."

Joseph nodded his head in agreement. "Let's get Leroy. He'll help us, especially after what they did to him last time they tried something."

The two of them went to the offices near the front of the facility where they found Susan talking to Leroy. Leroy faced Joseph and Franklin. "What's up?"

"We need to save Melissa and Dot," an excited Franklin exclaimed. "We know where they are. Let's go."

"Go where?" Susan fearfully asked.

"Nowhere," Leroy answered. "We can't leave this place. I'm the night attendant. I can't leave here. What if someone needs some help or something?"

"Susan's here," Joseph shouted. "She can take care of the place."

Leroy held up his hands. "Even if Susan stayed, what would we do? The best thing for us is to call the police and tell them where Melissa and Dot are."

"They already know," Joseph stated. "When Brenda's grandson called to tell us where they were, we told the two detectives who were waiting with us."

Leroy waved his hand to show his confusion. "How did he find out where they were?"

"Dot's emergency medical alarm thingy," Franklin proudly explained. "Melissa and Dot let themselves get kidnapped. When they found the killer's location, Dot pressed her emergency medical alarm button sending their location to the police. Brenda then called us so that we could go and rescue them. But we have to hurry and get there before the bad guys leave."

Leroy let out a deep breath. "No, we don't. The police are on their way there. They will rescue Melissa and Dot and get the bad guys. Us going after them will only cause problems. We're staying here."

Susan could see the look of disappointment on Joseph's and Franklin's faces.

∞∞∞∞∞∞

Haj instructed Smokey to take side roads after they left the old shoe factory. For ten minutes, Smokey snaked the van through the streets, following Haj's directions. Meanwhile, JJ and Theo ensured Dot and Melissa remained quiet in the back of the van.

"Pull in here," Haj demanded, pointing to a parking lot behind an apartment building. "Let me think for a moment."

"Sure thing," Smokey replied.

They sat for several minutes until JJ broke the silence. "What are we waiting for?"

"Thinking about what to do," Haj answered. "I still need that code and that copy of the notebook."

Smokey snickered. "The copy of the notebook is still at that old folks' home. It's locked in the manager's desk."

Haj smiled and patted Smokey on the shoulder. "Good idea. Start the car. I know where to go."

CHAPTER SIXTY-FIVE

Stanford drew his service weapon as he exited the vehicle. Cat did the same. Each one approached the entrance to the old shoe factory from the opposite sides of the door. They stopped at the entrance to listen for any sounds coming from inside. Their hope for a quiet entry was ruined when a car pulled up, focusing its headlights on the entrance. William, along with Jennifer and Brenda, got out of the car and ran up to the detectives.

"Have you found Melissa and Dot?" Jennifer shouted as she approached.

"No," Stanford hissed. "All of you stay back and out of the way. Cat and I will go in and check the place out. When patrol units get here, have them set up a perimeter around this place."

"I have a couple of buddies coming to help," William informed Stanford.

Stanford pointed a finger at William. "Everyone, and I mean everyone, stay out here. If we need help, we'll get backup from patrol units." Stanford didn't wait for a response. He and Cat entered the building.

"What are we going to do?" Brenda pleaded.

The plea was answered with the arrival of two patrol units, quickly followed by a third.

William walked over to the patrol officers. "I'm William Barlow with the fire department. Two detectives just went into the building. They told us to have you set up a perimeter of this building."

The senior patrol officer directed two of the units to go around to the back and cover any exits they find. He remained with William and the others. A fourth patrol unit arrived. With blue lights flashing, everyone waited.

A few minutes later, Stanford and Cat came out of the factory. "They're gone," Cat stated.

"But Dot was supposed to set her emergency medical alarm button off when she and Melissa were at the killer's hideout," Brenda said to the detectives.

"They must have known we were coming," Cat replied. "We found an emergency medical alarm button in there. Looks like they took off in a hurry."

Stanford turned to the senior patrol officer. "You and one other stay with us while we go through the scene. Have the others patrol the area to see if they can find anyone or anything."

Jennifer grabbed William's arm. "If they're gone, how are we going to find them?"

Stanford glared at Jennifer. "What you'll do is go home and let the police handle this. If you had brought us in from the beginning, maybe we would have found your two missing patients."

"Residents," Jennifer quietly corrected Stanford. "They are residents, not patients."

∞∞∞∞∞∞

"Don't cry," Brenda said, offering comfort from the back seat of the car to Jennifer who was sitting in the front passenger seat. "You didn't do anything wrong."

"It's all my fault," Jennifer said while sniffling and trying to hold back tears. "I thought that copy of the ledger would provide us protection. Instead, it got Melissa and Dot kidnapped. I will never forgive myself if they are harmed."

William glanced at the rearview mirror at Brenda before he reached over and patted Jennifer's shoulder. He spoke as he continued to drive. "It was a good plan. The problem was there was no backup. No one thought about what to do if there was a problem."

"So, now what do we do?" Brenda shouted. "We can't just give up."

"We go back to the home," William answered. "We go back and wait. It's up to the cops now." William pulled out his cell phone and passed it to Brenda. "Call Kevin and Dave. Let them know what happened and to meet us back at the home."

∞∞∞∞∞

William pulled into the parking lot of Comfort Cottages. Jennifer got out of the car and opened the door for Brenda. Jennifer held William's hand as he led her to the entrance. Normally, Brenda would be pleased to witness such a display of affection, but her concern for Melissa and Dot dominated her thoughts.

Franklin and Joseph were standing behind Leroy as he opened the door for William, Jennifer, and Brenda. "Did you rescue Melissa and Dot?" Franklin eagerly asked, pushing his way in front of Leroy.

"No," Jennifer answered with disappointment. "When we got there, the killers had already left. The police checked the place and found Dot's emergency medical alarm pennant. But they weren't there. I'm afraid they're in real danger, and there's nothing we can do to help them."

William reached over and gave Jennifer a gentle side hug. "Let's not think like that."

"That's right," Joseph asserted. "Melissa may be a bit snooty, but she's smart. And Dot has a lot of tricks up her sleeve. Those two will figure out some way to let us know where they are."

"I hope so," Jennifer replied trying to hold back tears. "We should have never become involved. I mean, who are we to try to find a killer. That's what the police do. Not a manager of an assisted living facility and its residents."

"What's wrong with us?" Franklin demanded. "I was a Marine. Just because we're old that doesn't mean we can't handle ourselves and catch a killer."

"Really?" a voice inquired. Everyone turned to see Melissa and Dot. Standing behind them were Haj along with Smokey, JJ, and Theo. "Well," Haj continued, "just how are you going to catch a killer?"

Franklin stepped forward and boastfully stated. "Well, we caught you, didn't we? Look, You're here. Now, you're under arrest."

Leroy put his hands on Franklin's arms and guided him to stand behind the others. "Franklin, why don't you let me handle this?"

"No," Franklin shouted, pointing at Haj. "He's the killer. He's the one I saw kill that woman. Look at those weird ears. See how they are bigger at the bottom than the top." Franklin again stepped to the front of the group. "You're under arrest. Put your hands on the wall and spread your feet."

Haj laughed and brought out a pistol. "You're tough old bird, ain't you?" He motioned for Melissa and Dot to join the others. Behind Haj stood JJ, Theo, and Smokey. Less than six feet in front of Haj, were Leroy, William, and the others.

Leroy held up his hands. "Hey, let's calm down. Just what do you want?"

Haj moved closer to Leroy. "First, I want that copy you have of the notebook that you gave Smokey."

William stepped in front of Jennifer, moving her back and hoping the man with the pistol wouldn't notice. "Then what?" he asked.

"He's going to kill us," Melissa answered. "He can't let us go because we can identify him. But he's got a problem. It used to be just Franklin who knew he killed that girl. Now, it's all of us."

"He can't kill all of us," Leroy stated. "Think about it. There are nine of us standing here. At the first shot, other residents will come out to see what's happening. I doubt he has enough bullets. Then there are his buddies. When they are caught, it's guaranteed at least one of them will turn on him. No one wants to go down for a mass shooting. No. Shooting us will only make things worse."

"Wait a minute," Smokey shouted. "No one said anything about shooting anyone. You told me you only wanted the copy of the notebook and how to decipher it."

"Quiet!" Haj commanded. He took a step back, pointing his pistol at Leroy. "Think you're pretty smart. Maybe I'll shoot you just to prove a point. What do you say to that?"

"No!" Smokey shouted again. "Don't shoot anybody. Just get the copy and let's get out of here."

"What about the old man?" JJ asked. "He can identify Haj."

Leroy smirked. "Freaky Franky suffers from dementia. Come tomorrow, he'll probably forget you were even here tonight."

JJ jabbed Leroy in the chest. "But you won't forget."

"No, I won't."

"Well, Boy," JJ said in a derogatory tone as he pulled out a revolver. "Then you had better do what I tell you, hadn't you?"

Leroy glared at JJ. JJ smiled. He had control of the situation and he enjoyed being able to insult and anger the black man standing in front of him.

"Knock it off," Haj told JJ. "Get that copy of the ledger."

"Sure thing," JJ replied. He motioned with his revolver to Leroy. "Come on, Boy. You go and get the ledger. And remember, I'll be right behind you." JJ followed Leroy into Jennifer's office.

∞∞∞∞∞∞

Kevin convinced David that they needed to stop off at Walmart and pick up some donuts and cookies before heading back to Comfort Cottages to meet up with William, his grandmother, and Jennifer. They were about to open the front door of the facility when they saw a white man forcing Leroy into Jennifer's office. Kevin made sure to carefully place the donuts and cookies in a chair, and waited until the two men were in the office and out of sight before he opened the front door for David and him to enter the building.

They moved quietly toward the office. David picked up a fire extinguisher, the only thing he could use as a weapon against the man with the pistol. They were almost to the office when Theo spotted them.

Theo turned to confront the two firefighters. Without hesitation, David lifted the nozzle of the fire extinguisher and released the chemicals into Theo's face. Kevin leaned down and pulled Theo's legs from under him.

The noise of David's attack made JJ turn to see what was happening. Leroy took the opportunity to grab a can of air freshener with one hand and spray JJ's eyes as he grabbed JJ's hand that had the revolver and twisted JJ's arm. Leroy slammed JJ's hand against the edge of the desk, knocking the pistol from his hand. Then with great satisfaction, Leroy punched JJ in the face, knocking him to the ground.

The fire extinguisher attack distracted Haj. William charged him. The pistol in Haj's hand went off, but William's momentum carried him forward knocking Haj on his back.

Franklin willed his legs to carry him forward. He grabbed a chair. Haj pushed William off him, but before he could get up, Franklin brought the chair down on Haj. He kicked Haj twice as Haj tried to aim his pistol at his attacker. Franklin brought the chair down on Haj's arm, breaking in and forcing Haj to release the pistol.

The pistol slid a few feet away from Haj. Jennifer lunged for the weapon and picked it up.

Joseph and Brenda joined Franklin in kicking and stomping on Haj.

"Back away," Jennifer shouted. Franklin, Joseph, and Brenda backed away from Haj. Kevin and David also moved aside. This left Haj and Theo on the ground. Jennifer leveled the pistol at Haj. "If either one of you moves, I'll shoot."

Haj chuckled. "You don't have the balls."

Kevin took the pistol from Jennifer and stepped back, ensuring there was at least six feet between him and the two men on the ground. He motioned for everyone to get behind him. "She may not, but I do. And for your information, two tours in Afghanistan taught me how to shoot with a great deal of accuracy."

Jennifer saw William bleeding. She rushed to him. Leroy came out of Jennifer's office, pushing JJ in front. He saw Kevin with a pistol, covering Haj and Theo. "Here's another one for you," Leroy said as he handed the pistol he had taken for JJ to David. "Watch them. I'll get the first aid kit and take care of William." Leroy pointed to Jennifer. "You call for an ambulance and the police."

Melissa looked around. "Oh, my goodness. Where's Smokey? In all the confusion, he's run away."

"No, I haven't," a voice shouted. Smokey ran over with the first aid kit and handed it to Leroy. "By the way, I also called the police and EMTs." Leroy grabbed the kit and began administering first aid to William.

Melissa walked up to Smokey. "Why didn't you run?"

Smokey shrugged his shoulders. "I don't know. Maybe it's because I was pissed that Haj killed my friend, Denise. Maybe because I didn't want to see you or anyone else get hurt. All I wanted was that notebook and the copy of it so that my grandma and me would be left alone."

"And you knew that was never going to happen," Melissa replied.

"What's going to happen now?" Smokey asked.

Melissa looked over to the front of the building where she could see red and blue flashing lights. "First, we take care of Brenda's grandson. Then, we let the police deal with these three, and I'm sorry to say, what you have done." Melissa reached over and grasped Smokey's hand. "But know this, we'll be there to help you through it."

CHAPTER SIXTY-SIX

Stanford looked at Cat and let out a deep breath. "It's going to be a long night."

"Gee, do you think," Cat replied. "We have four suspects in custody. A gunshot victim with two firefighter heroes, who are at the hospital with the victim. Then, there are the witnesses we have here. And keeping them separated is like controlling three-year-olds in a candy store."

Stanford and Cat walked into the dining room where Leroy, Dot, Melissa, Franklin, and Joseph were waiting with two patrol officers trying to keep them apart. The patrol officers had strung crime scene tape across half of the room to keep the other residents away from the four witnesses seated at four different tables. While everyone was physically separated, they continued to talk across the room to each other.

"Quiet!" Stanford bellowed. "We need to interview each witness separately, and without any help or comments from anyone else."

Melissa stood up. "May I make a suggestion. Each one of us could go to our rooms. We would be alone and you could interview us privately. To ensure we are alone, you could have the patrol officers in the hall. Our rooms are close enough together that they could easily do that."

Joseph also stood up. "Well, I'm not moving until I know what's happened to Brenda's grandson and the killers."

Cat stepped forward. "I understand your concern. The four suspects are in custody and were transported to the police station. Mr. William Barlow was taken to the hospital. His grandmother, along with Ms. Stebbins, are at the hospital with him. The two firefighters who were here also went to the hospital with their friend. As soon as we hear anything about Mr. Barlow's condition, we will tell you. Now, Detective Agusta and I need you to go to your rooms and wait for us."

The patrol officers pulled down the crime scene tape and directed the four witnesses to the hallway leading to their rooms. The other residents in the dining room made a corridor for the witnesses and police officers to pass.

∞∞∞∞∞

Brenda and Jennifer jumped to their feet when Dr. Robinson came into the waiting room. Kevin and David rushed forward to hear what the doctor had to say.

The doctor approached Brenda. "Ms. Elson, I have good news. Your grandson came through the surgery without any problems. He's young and strong, so I expect him to make a full recovery, although he's going to be laid up for a while."

"By the way," Dr. Robinson said as he faced Jennifer. "The other gunshot victim, that woman you said who worked for you. She's doing much better. She'll probably be released in a day or two. But she will need some care once she's released."

Jennifer sighed with relief. "Not a problem. I'll make sure both Freya and William get the best home care available."

The doctor began to turn away, but stopped and faced the four individuals in front of him. "One other thing, we got a call from the police and they asked for you all to go to the police station in the morning to give them your statements. I'm sure it's just a formality." The doctor gave them a wave before leaving.

"Well, I think we should go home and get some sleep before we have to go down to the police station," Kevin suggested. "Do you want David and me to give you two a ride.

"No," Brenda stubbornly declared. "I'm staying here with my grandson."

Kevin looked at Jennifer. "What about you?"

Brenda wrapped her arm around Jennifer's arm. "She's staying too."

Jennifer grasped Brenda's arm. "You heard the lady. We're staying."

David chuckled. "Then, I guess we'll see you in the morning." The two firemen gave Jennifer and Brenda a salute before leaving.

CHAPTER SIXTY-SEVEN
(two days later— day eighteen)

Brenda and Jennifer entered William's hospital room. William was sitting up in his bed. Jennifer's attention was drawn between William and the monitors next to his bed. Jennifer walked over and sat on the edge of his bed. "So, how are you feeling today?"

William raised his hand, waved it to show he was okay, then lowered it again. "Considering I was shot two days ago, I guess I'm doing okay."

Jennifer patted William's leg. "According to the doctors, you're going to make a complete recovery, although it will be a while before you're going to be fighting fires again."

"Well, I'm just glad no one else was injured," Brenda interjected. "If it hadn't been for your two friends showing up when they did, who knows what would have happened."

Jennifer pulled her hand away before staring at William. "I was terrified. We had this plan and it failed. Then we end up at Comfort Cottages with a gang of killers. I'm glad your friends showed up."

"What happened to the bad guys?" William asked as he pushed himself up a little bit more on his bed.

Jennifer let out a loud sigh. "Quite a bit. I guess I should start with that night. Brenda and I rode in the ambulance with you to the hospital. Several hours later, the surgeon came out and told us you made it through surgery. It was almost three in the morning before I got home. After a few hours of sleep, I met Brenda at the police station to give them our statements. We found out that all of them, including Smokey, were in jail awaiting charges."

"What happens when they get out on bail?" Brenda asked unable to hide the anxiety in her voice.

Jennifer patted Brenda's hand. "I talked to Detective Agusta Smokey will probably be released on bail. Melissa knows the judge and she thinks she can get him released to his grandmother, but he'll be wearing an ankle monitor and basically under house arrest. The others will probably be denied bail. Turns out the one called Haj killed the woman at Barnyard Barbecue. He's also a suspect in another homicide Smokey identified the other two as the ones who broke into Comfort Cottages that night. Freya identified them as the ones who shot her. Then there was that night when they kidnapped Dot and Melissa, along with holding all of us hostage. So, I'm sure there is no way any of them are getting bail."

"What about that ledger everyone wanted?" William asked. "They went through a lot of trouble to get it."

"That was a record of the money Haj collected," Jennifer answered. "The woman Haj killed created it as a form of insurance against him. It also incriminated another individual known as the Accountant. He controlled a large money laundering network. One of his henchmen was captured when the police rescued Smokey's grandmother. He managed to get bail, and he's gone. No one knows where he is, as well as the whereabouts of the Accountant."

William pointed to Jennifer. "Should I be jealous? You seem to be awfully friendly with this detective."

Jennifer stood up and turned her back to William. She took a few steps forward before turning and looking over her left shoulder. "Maybe."

"Quit teasing him," Brenda said, waving her hand at Jennifer. Brenda faced William. "Detective Agusta came over yesterday and told us everything before he and Franklin took off to a ball game." Brenda placed her hand on William's. "Now you just worry about getting better."

"I don't know," William responded. "I'm going to need a lot of TLC when I get out of the hospital."

Brenda smiled at Jennifer. "Don't worry," Brenda said. "I happened to know you're going to have a wonderful nurse taking care of you."

THE END

About the Author

Mark Zeid spent seven years on active duty as a military police officer for the U.S. Marine Corps. After the Marines, he went to college and grad school, which led him to working and living in Japan for 25 years. During which time he taught English for Japanese schools and criminal justice for a satellite college on military bases. He also published more than 600 articles in various military, educational, and local news publications. Mark Zeid retired from the Marine Corps Reserves in 2004. Upon returning to the United States, he worked at the Center for Domestic Preparedness, a training facility run by Homeland Security for first responders. He was deployed several times to help with disaster recovery efforts in the United States. Currently retired, Mark Zeid teaches writing classes and Holocaust education.

His novels are inspired by actual criminal events. He has had four mystery novels published, two of which won local awards. He publishes the first chapter of his novels on his website at https://zeidsmysteries.com

Thank you for reading.
Please review this book. Reviews help others find
Absolutely Amazing eBooks and inspire us to keep
providing these marvelous tales.
If you would like to be put on our email list to receive
updates on new releases, contests, and promotions, please
go to AbsolutelyAmazingEbooks.com and sign up.

AbsolutelyAmazingEbooks.com

or AA-eBooks.com

For sales, editorial information, subsidiary rights information
or a catalog, please write or phone or e-mail
AbsolutelyAmazingEbooks
Manhanset House
Shelter Island Hts., New York 11965-0342, US
Tel: 212-427-7139
www.AbsolutelyAmazingEbooks.com
bricktower@aol.com
www.IngramContent.com

For sales in the UK and Europe please contact our distributor,
Gazelle Book Services
White Cross Mills
Lancaster, LA1 4XS, UK
Tel: (01524) 68765 Fax: (01524) 63232
email: jacky@gazellebooks.co.uk